Better Days

Carys Reed

Published by Carys Reed, 2023.

BETTER DAYS

First edition. January 13, 2023.

ISBN: 979-8215463505

Written by Carys Reed.

Better Days

By Carys Reed
Copyright 2023 Carys Reed
Published by Carys Reed

Note to reader: this is a clean version of a previously published contemporary romance novel under a different pen name of mine. I've remastered it and created a pen name that writes strictly clean romance: Carys Reed. Clean, meaning no profanity or sexual scenes.

Chapter One

From behind sheer ivory drapes, my gaze flows out across the orchard to the sky. It's a gorgeous sunny day with just enough cloud to make the humidity bearable—it's the perfect day for our annual Labor Day-slash-Pre-Harvest Barbecue.

The sight before me catches my breath, always. Like giant sentries, the pecan trees create waves of lush greens as far as the eye can see. We'll have a healthy harvest this year. I can't wait to be part of it, all of it, including our peanut harvest which will soon be underway.

I'm living my dream, and it brings a smile to my lips.

My eyes catch Ms. Donnelly sashaying from her car to the front porch with her arm hooked through that of a handsome middle-aged fellow—must be the latest in a long line of beaus since her divorce a few years back. She's wearing the cutest yellow sundress, a matching hat, and a beaming smile that invites everyone to admire her latest arm candy. They're all looking too, and they're dressed for a day of the finest catered barbecue in all of Alabama accompanied by the latest and juiciest gossip.

They'll be gossiping about me, and the thought makes my skin crawl.

This year's celebration is quickly becoming the bane of my existence. It's been coming for months, and I've dreaded every second. I've managed to avoid most socials this past few years, but now that I've graduated college, I'm fair game and will be at the mercy of every Southern busybody in attendance.

The whole party is really an ambush. Mamma and her circle have made it their mission to pair me up, because God forbid a lady of my stature is single with no visible prospects for a husband in the near vicinity.

Ugh.

If I have to listen to one more person question my life choices, I'm going to scream. I mean, what century do we live in?

What are your plans now that you've graduated from college?
Don't you get lonely on the farm?
A lady doesn't get her hands so dirty.
Are you seeing anyone special?
How do you expect to meet someone if you're cooped up on the farm all the time?

Oh, and let's not forget those that immediately feel they should set me up with their nearest available male relative the moment they find out I'm single.

She'll never get married.
She'll never have children.
She needs a steady boyfriend.
Blah, blah, blah.

This is *my* life, and I have every intention of living it here on our land, growing pecans and peanuts and whatever else we want. This land is my little slice of Heaven, my everything. The devoted husband and adorable children that fill our home will come in due time. I refuse to rush. I'm only twenty-two.

"Zeta, darling," Mamma says, rushing into my room. Turning to greet her, I smile—she's stunning in her designer lilac dress, cut from the finest silk. It's her favorite fabric and by her claim it's the cooling quality of it, but I know better; it's about presentation, the status wearing such finery boasts. "You must come downstairs and greet our guests. Come on, darling."

I'm trapped and she knows it. What I wouldn't give to just close the door and hide out under the covers with a flashlight and a good book. Turning my head away, I clear my throat and release a hard eye roll of contention, out of Mamma's sight. Her hand reaches out to me, I take it, turn, and feign a smile. She has me exactly where she wants me and laughs that bubbly infectious sound that both acknowledges her true plan and forces my mood to lighten.

"Mamma, thank you for putting together what I'm sure is going to be a phenomenal party..." She knows I see through her charade, and I know she's invited every family in the county with available sons, but I'm grateful for the time and planning she put into it. Her heart is pure gold and I know she would do and has done anything for me, my entire life. She'll take any opportunity to show off her only child. This woman is my heart. I'm truly blessed to have such a loving mamma.

"Pish posh, darling. It's just a celebration of another soon-to-be fruitful harvest," she says with a saucy wink as a mischievous half-grin curves her pink lips. "Before you know it, the guests will be gone, and you'll be an old maid trapped on this land with Daddy and I."

"Oh, I can't wait." Truly, I can't. The introvert in me is giddy with the thought of it, although I'm sure Mamma just cringed. She'd prefer I were more social, and I know she prays to the good Lord above that her only daughter would take an interest in the debutante season.

Ugh. No thanks.

Somehow, I've managed not to get sucked into *that* craziness. I can't parade around like I'm all that and then some—I can't stand being the center of attention, so this day is going to be loads of fun.

Mamma is the very definition of socialite—she lives and breathes the Mystic Ladies and all the parties and planning and charities. It's a rare sight to see Mamma venture into the orchard, but I routinely get lost in it. She certainly doesn't dig her hands into the earth and hates that I do, but because she loves me, it is never an issue. I'm sure she prays every day that my trajectory veers off into the direction of dating and marriage.

"You know," Mamma drawls. Oh no, here it comes, again. "Branson Montgomery just graduated, too." The way she croons the word *too* tells me exactly what's coming next. "He just returned from a trip to Europe and is anxious to see you. His family would love if ours..."

"Mamma!" I snap, my feet digging in at the bedroom door. "You didn't." I know she did. Of course, she did. 'Anxious to see me,' *Uh-huh*. Branson *Junior* would be at the top of her list of suitors.

"Well, of course, I invited them—they're practically family, and they're staying the weekend. Daddy has business with Branson Senior." She sings it like Scarlet O'Hara as if the lie just might be the truth. It's all a convenient setup. Business. *right*.

"They're staying the weekend?" I croak, not even trying to disguise my disappointment. The smile on her face tells me all I need to know.

"I'm sure, your daddy and Mr. Montgomery have so much to discuss. We'll wrap it up with a formal dinner tomorrow night and then we're heading into a meeting and will be staying the night at their house." She nudges me as if hoping her excitement will somehow rub off on me. "It's been ages since we've seen Branson Junior—you both have some catching up to do. Oh, I *do* hope you two marry, one day..." And there it is, the reason for all the extra effort she put into planning this year's barbecue. There's no point in fighting her. She's playing matchmaker. Always. It's a Southern mamma thing.

Two whole days and two whole nights. I would literally rather die than spend the entire weekend entertaining, but that is exactly what I will be doing.

Branson.

Pfft.

An eyebrow lifts, challenging Mamma. "I can't believe y'all think an arranged marriage is logical—what century do we live in again?"

"My goodness!" Her attempt to appear appalled isn't even slightly convincing. "It's not *arranged.* You're so dramatic, darling. It's your choice—it would just be lovely if the two of you...*connected.*"

"We've played together since we were babies."

"I meant romantically, and you know it. I only want what's best for you and marrying Branson would ensure you're looked after. You're friends, it's only natural..."

I'm fairly certain that the only thing between Branson and I is friendship. I've never thought otherwise. This is my fate now—I know this won't be the end of it, either. I wish she would hear me and trust that I can *absolutely* take care of myself. I don't know, I think she just really wants grandchildren, like *really* wants them, and as soon as possible.

Interesting how the concept of falling in love doesn't even enter the equation. Mamma and Lydia Montgomery are best friends, so they've been praying their only babies would marry since the day we were born. Branson and I have been at the mercy of their matchmaking for as long as I can remember, so this is nothing new.

Branson's decent enough, and I've always considered him a friend, but falling in love with him doesn't feel the least bit natural. I haven't seen him in years, since we went off to different colleges—He could be a different person, he could be like his *dad*. I shudder on the inside.

Mamma sighs, straightening, plastering her game-face on. "Enough of that, we have guests to entertain." She fluffs her shoulder-length mahogany curls and then eyes me, clearly wondering how to make her daughter more appealing. Reaching out with both hands, she swoops my mid-length blonde locks off my shoulder so they're hanging perfectly down my back. As she snatches her hands back, her bold brown eyes assess me with pride, and I swear they almost look glassy. She's such a softy.

Returning her smile, I play along, displaying my manners in true Southern Belle fashion. It's only a weekend, and I'd do anything for this woman.

We descend the stairs and Daddy and Branson Junior, the object of my Mamma's affection and supposedly should be mine, are waiting. The party is in full swing, the main level of our home invaded with half the county and many from Mobile all crammed inside happy to take up the cooler air.

Branson half bows and nods with an adorable grin. His short brown hair looks freshly barbered, pristine, no doubt meant to display the clean-cut perfection his daddy exhibits, at all times—I swear that man has no idea what it means to relax. Branson is the spitting image of his daddy, only kinder, and it shows in his beaming blue eyes.

At least he's kind of hot. I could do worse. I'm no pooch, but I find myself wondering if I look decent—Mamma bought this dress for me, and although I love the pale blue fabric, I worry it makes me look too prim.

Like he's reading my mind, and as if he's trying to ease my troubled thoughts, Branson says, "Zeta, you're looking lovely. It's nice to see you after all these years."

My reply is interrupted by an incoming busybody—the first in what will no doubt be a long line of them.

"*Yoo-hoo*," Ms. Donnelly coos as she pushes her way into our awkward little circle with her beau still tightly linked by the arm. My body stiffens in response to what I know comes next. "How are you, darling. My son, Johnny is on his way, he's an intern at..."

And that is literally how the next two hours pass me by: one person after another, taking shots at me with polite smiles plastered on their faces as they make every attempt to nose around my business, set me up with their offspring, invite me to meetings, or flirt with me. I feel like the barbecue on the buffet table.

By late afternoon, I'm exhausted, fed up, and desperate for escape. I spot Branson Junior off to the side, at the mercy of Ms. Donnelly, who is no doubt pitching the perfections of her daughter Cleo to him. Ms. Donnelly has four children—her work won't be done until all are married with children. Branson's brow looks strained as he tries to hold a veil of politeness in place. Sure, he's about as done with all the shenanigans as I am, I make my move.

I approach, grab Branson's hand, and smile huge. "I'm so sorry to interrupt, Ms. Donnelly, but Branson promised me a walk." I give his hand a squeeze of solidarity. I turn to see Mamma approaching and rush to explain myself. "Oh, I know it's rude of me to leave the party, but Branson and I have much to discuss."

The smile on Mamma's face beams but her eyes squint just so, indicating that she's on to me. She won't let on, though. "Of course, my darling. You and Branson run along but mind you're back for dinner in an hour."

Branson clears his throat and nods. "Yes, ma'am. It was a pleasure seeing you again, Ms. Donnelly. Now, if you don't mind, I'm about to escort this lovely lady on a tour of the orchard."

Ms. Donnelly smiles and changes gears, spinning as she drags her beau off in search of a new victim. Branson and I excuse ourselves and head out. I swear Mamma would squeal with glee if she weren't surrounded by guests.

Chapter Two

I've never been so happy to escape my home. As Branson and I bust through the front door and make our way through the trees, I'm blissfully aware of my freedom. It's been years since we've seen each other, our only contact being the odd banter via social media. We've lost touch, not that we were besties or anything, but this still feels awkward.

We walk in silence for a few minutes while I take in this land that will be mine one day. The clear blue sky, the fresh floral scent of Mamma's precious encore azaleas rolling off our gardens, the birds chirping in the trees, the clean, quiet country air—my home, this oasis is as close to heavenly as it can possibly get.

It's late afternoon and no cooler than midday—it's the kind of heat that feels like you've been slapped with a hot wet towel. Normally, I'd stay indoors until it cools just slightly, but there is no way I'm going back into that party until barbecue is served. Besides, the heat doesn't bother me in my light sundress and sandals, and if we stick to the orchard, there'll be plenty of shade.

My head swivels, and I scan Branson's attire. He must be dying. "Branson, what possessed you to wear those Chinos and dress shirt? You must be roasting." He's dressed college prep and looks out of place, starchy, ridiculous.

"My mamma is every bit as overbearing as yours." He laughs.

"Touché." Shaking my head, I grin. "You'll be joining your daddy's firm now that you're done travelling?"

"I guess so." I sense him stiffen next to me. His daddy is a touchy subject.

"You don't sound very excited about it," I say, acknowledging his tight demeanor.

"Believe me, I'm not excited about selling insurance, but you know how it is, Dad would be crushed if I chose to work someplace else." The way he says it makes my stomach flip. He won't say the words out loud, but it's likely Mr. Montgomery is bullying his son into working at the firm—I highly doubt the man would be crushed, but he'll make his son's life a living hell if he doesn't get his way.

Sighing, I shake my head and stop, standing hand on hip as I turn to him. "Why do you let him control you, still?"

He shrugs, a silly grin curves his lips. "Mamma..."

Rolling my eyes, I laugh. In the end, daddies don't have a say, not really. It's always our mammas that get the last word, and we'd do just about anything for them. "Yup. Mammas...So mine still thinks you and I should get married," I say, tilting my head to the side as I gage his reaction. I mean, why beat around the bush? I'm curious what he thinks, and I know beyond all doubt that his mamma has put a bug in his ear. Our mammas are like two peas in a pod.

"Would it be so bad?" He's straight-faced, aside from a slight lopsided grin.

Taken aback, my body jolts with surprise as my cheeky facade fades along with the color in my face. I snap my gaping jaw shut. I hadn't expected him to be on board with it—he never has been before. "*Seriously?*" My voice squeaks with disbelief.

He's smirking, ignoring my terrible reaction to his words. "Sure. I mean, why not? I think our parents might have the best examples of marriage I've ever seen. They're kind to each other, loving, they're a team, and they weren't in love when they married."

"First of all, *my* parents *were* in love when they got married—I can't speak for your parents. Maybe back in the day, arranged marriages were a thing, but not now...Is that what you want? To marry someone, you're not in love with?" Debating this is insane, and I'm surprised he's entertaining the notion—I can't believe anyone would.

"I'd rather marry a woman who's decent looking and kind, and who has a booming business that I am interested in, than spend the next forty years working in my Dad's firm and married to some cow." The way he bitterly blurts it out, stuns me. My mouth falls open and my eyes bulge. "Besides, love, like respect and admiration, would grow, and is it really *arranged* if we both go into the marriage willingly?"

"*Um*, yeah, it is...I...I can't believe you just said all that," I stutter, beyond dumbfounded. We couldn't be further apart on this issue.

"We should be honest with each other if we're going to get married." He winks, and his tone is teasing, so I relax and giggle.

"Well," I turn, nudging him with my shoulder before walking away. "Thanks for the offer, but I think I'm going to pass. I intend to marry for love, not business."

"I don't know, it seems like a logical choice." Does he legit think this is a rational decision?

"Yeah but being in love isn't logical—it just...*is*."

"I wouldn't know," he says, and it sounds like he doesn't even want to know. I think that's what bothers me most. How can you not want love?

"Well, someday, *I'd* like to know. I can't talk about this anymore. It's too ridiculous, but just to torture our parents, I think we should spend the weekend hanging out."

"You mean, avoiding them." Point blank range.

"Yup." My smile widens—no denying it.

"*And* Ms. Donnelly?" he says.

"You catch on fast." I laugh, happy to have a partner in crime.

Branson stops walking, so I do the same and turn to him, curious. His eyes search mine, like he wants to say something but doesn't know how to get the words out. He reaches out and tugs me into his arms, crashing his lips to mine. It's quick, and although I'm caught off guard by this bold move, there isn't a single spark—no...*excitement*.

He pulls away, drops his arms and watches me. My eyebrow raises as I prop a hand on hip. "Really, Branson?"

"Just curious as to how my wife might kiss...Wow!" He huffs, seemingly impressed with what I considered a disappointment.

Rolling my eyes, I give him a playful shove and continue to walk, hoping to forget the kiss. If I had to place it, I'd say that kiss sits nicely at the bottom of my kiss list. Not that the list is long, it's now sitting at three, because I haven't really dated. Still, it just felt wrong. It's a good thing he kissed me though, because now I know we are *never* getting married. There's zero attraction here—no fuzzy feels whatsoever. Shouldn't that be a given?

Our parents are nuts, we both recognize this, but I get the distinct feeling Branson is desperate to get out from under his daddy's thumb and will do whatever it takes. I don't blame him. Mr. Montgomery is gruff, old-school, and a total unapologetic jerk. The way he talks to his son makes me cringe, but I'm not running off with Branson just to save his soul. Pity is no way to start a marriage, and other than friendship, it's the only feeling I have for Branson.

From behind me, he yells while running to catch up. "You'll make a fine wife, Zeta Reilly." He's laughing while he bodychecks me, and we continue to walk.

At least he's a nice guy, a friend.

But I'm absolutely *not* going to marry him.

We make our way back to the party, arriving just in time for dinner. Rows of tables have been set up in the yard under the shade of magnolia trees, and the buffet table is overflowing with barbecue and all the fixings. Dozens of guests, and most of the workers are present, lining up at the buffet to fill their plates.

I leave Branson with his parents and make my way to mine. Taking a seat next to Daddy, we watch, equally content, happily observing our most important people as they prepare to celebrate the upcoming harvest with us.

My eyes scan the line of workers, who always get to eat first, and pride washes over me. No matter how Mamma tries to spin it in her most devious ways, this barbecue is in honor of the workers and all they do. We have a fantastic crew, but none of this would be possible without them.

It's then that I see *him*—tall, tanned, muscular, and dreamy. The kind of wow that really hits home. His thick dark hair, in need of a trim, cascading across his forehead, that white T-shirt snuggly highlighting the washboard abs beneath it, and the jovial smile on his face as he chats with those in line next to him. He's radiant, the most beautiful man I've ever seen.

"Zeta, darling, come and get some food," Mamma says as she steps in front of my line of sight. Snapping out of it, I rise, prepared to follow her—mostly I'm curious and need to find out who that man is, but when Mamma moves out of the way, and I look over to where he was standing, he is gone.

Did I dream it?

Scanning the yard, I don't see him, so I must have, but *oh*, what a dream!

Chapter Three

The weekend's been two days of constant smiling, entertaining Branson, and too many people for my liking. I crave the quiet. We've finally wrapped up an early dinner with the Montgomery clan, and Daddy announces they're heading out. They'll be dropping Branson off at home and attending a function in Mobile.

Since it's a sixty-mile drive, they'll be spending the night. I'm having difficulty masking my disappointment. I hoped to spend the evening stargazing with Daddy. It's the perfect night for it, but it wouldn't be the same on my own.

Like he reads my mind, Daddy says, "We'll be home tomorrow, and then you and I will head out tomorrow night." He pulls me into a hug, kissing the side of my head. As we pull apart, he winks and smirks, his blue eyes conveying the truth: He's about as done with all this entertaining as I am.

Mamma leans in to kiss my cheek and then links her arm through daddy's as they walk out the door. Ecstatic, I'm going to have the house to myself, I follow them out and say my goodbyes, my smile genuine this time because the opportunity to relax is welcome.

With the whole house to myself, I race upstairs to my room and grab a book and blanket. The late afternoon sky is clear, perfect for stargazing, and I'm looking forward to getting out there tomorrow. In the meantime, I'm going to chill on the porch with a good read. I snuggle into the papasan swing and become one with my story, losing myself between the pages.

At some point, movement off between the trees catches my eye. Glancing up, I realize it's dark, I've lost all track of time, and I can't make out the person. The light from the porch doesn't reach far enough, so I squint, wondering who's entering the orchard at this hour. I'm sure it's one of the summer hires, one of the many students that come to work here each summer while saving money for college. The last of the students should be heading back to college this week.

Curious, I arch a brow and drop my book, deciding to check it out. He could be up to no good, or maybe he's lost. He's a long way off from the worker cabins, and it can be difficult to navigate the land through the trees in the dark.

The nosy Southerner in me rises to the surface. I follow him, keeping a distance between us as he continues ahead of me, walking the path between the trees. It's too dark, and I'm having difficulty making out his form. A piece of me prays it's the man from the barbecue, the one I thought I imagined. I speed up but then he's gone.

Where did he go?

Pausing, I scan the area. He's vanished, and now I'm questioning my sanity. Am I seeing people that aren't really there? Turning to head back, I'm startled out of my skin when someone moves out from between the trees and appears right before me. The screech that escapes my lips causes him to jump back. It's dark, but there is enough light for me to clearly make out his face.

Sweet baby Jesus.

It's him.

Those hard, chiseled cheekbones lined with the shadow of stubble—just enough actually. The way his dark hair swoops lazily across his brow is beyond captivating. He's *stunning*. He's real all right, I *didn't* imagine him. But where did he come from? How did I not see him around?

How is it that someone I don't even know can have such an immediate effect on me? I'm focusing hard, trying to maintain a straight expression, to not give away these crazy thoughts.

"Why are you following me?" he asks, a definite tease to his tone.

Oh, he totally realizes his effect on me.

I can't have that.

"*Um*, I...thought maybe you were lost...You're a summer hire, right?" I try to sound less like a stalker and more casual, but I'm pretty sure that ship has sailed.

"Yeah. Just taking a walk. It's a nice night." He turns and walks away. Flustered, I stare after him, my curiosity, among other things, more than a little aroused. It's perplexing, completely unusual, yet also welcome. "You can join me if you like..."

I shouldn't. I don't know this man, but my legs take over, and I race to catch up to him. "I'm Zeta," I say.

"I know who you are. Your family owns this land—It's more like a small country." He stops, turns to me, and eyes me. "Where to? You grew up here, where should someone go to think?"

"Well, normally I'd head straight for the farthest edge of the orchard, where the trees stop and the fields begin—it's where I usually go to stargaze, but my telescope is back at the house. The greenhouse is the next best thing—the budding life, the flowers, it's very relaxing and a lot less buggy." Words just tumble from my lips, and I'm sure I sound stupid, like a blubbering fool.

He makes a sweeping motion with his arm, and I nod, leading the way. "I'm Nick," he says.

We walk to the green house in silence. Once inside, I stroll along the isles, making no move to turn on a light. "It's better in the dark. I have just the spot."

At the back of the greenhouse, an area of loungers and chairs are set up. It's one of my favorite places. Nick plops himself into a lounger and stares up through the screened roof at the night sky. He doesn't speak, so I recline in the lounger next to him and do the same.

"I've only been here in the daylight, but this is pretty awesome," he says.

"Right? The roof in this area is just screened in, so it's very open and the perfect place to chill and watch the stars."

He sighs audibly, and it's laced with frustration.

"What's got you so stressed?" Why did I ask? It's none of my business.

"College, life, you know..."

I laugh. "Yup I know, and I'm happy to be done with it—with college, I mean." My voice quakes with nervousness and the thumping in my chest is insane. Why do I feel so uncomfortable? Closing my eyes, I silently beg my racing heart to calm while focusing hard on my words. "You're returning to college this week, right?"

"Yup. Classes start in two days—I need to pick up a couple to complete my degree."

"What's your major?"

"Business, but I'd rather be in biology, botany. My parents insist I use my education to its full potential." His tone is sarcastic, very bitter with just a hint of resolve.

"Is that why you're working here? To gain experience?"

"Yeah. Some of us weren't born into money." The dryness to his tone upsets me because I now feel unfairly judged.

Fire rises to the surface, blushing my cheeks and causing me to snap back as I shoot him a death glare. "Excuse me, I'm not some spoiled rich brat, you know. I do have a mind, and I intend to use it and *never* squander what I've been born into. *Jeez*, people assume that just because we have money that we're worse than the devil. My father, my father's father, my entire family has worked their fingers to the bone to get here. *Nothing* has been handed to us. It's all earned, and we're good people, my parents are so kind and generous. Not cool, Nick, not cool." There's a definite pout to my lip and I'm trying to rein it in, to stop the tears that threaten to fall.

"I never meant...Well, yeah, I meant it." He chuckles, shaking his head. "I apologize. I wasn't trying to be cruel though, just meaning I have to work harder to find my place in the world, too. It's no disrespect, you're just lucky is all."

His words help, and yes, I overreacted, but I can't stand being judged. I get where he's coming from though, so I calm. "I *am* lucky, blessed actually, and I know it. God put me exactly where I am meant to be. Mamma says I have mud running through my veins, that I was born to be a farmer. She hates it, wishes I were more interested in the debutante ways. I love this life, the dirt beneath my nails, the hard work—just being a part of it is truly amazing."

"I feel the same—the land, the trees, making something flourish—you're right, it's amazing." His tone is dreamy. All previous and overreactive rage dissolves with the sound of it, but my heart still races.

If I could just relax, this could be a fantastic conversation because I am one-hundred-percent intrigued with this man and his love of the land that aligns with my own. I feel safe in this space, so I say, "Out here, day or night, the beauty makes me feel connected to our world, our universe, in a much deeper way. I'd take an orchard full of trees over a stuffy office job any day."

"Agreed. I'm going to run an orchard one day." His confident tone states he will do just that.

"Well then, you should ask our orchard manager, Clive, to mentor you when you finish college. He's one of the best there is. We're so lucky to have him."

"I'll do that. Thanks."

We lay in silence, taking in the air around us. Mine is clogged with questions about what to do next. I'm trying to be casual, but I'm too awkward. Nick is *really* hot, and I'm so lame when it comes to dating, flirting. I'm too straightforward for games and have no idea how to act.

"Word in the field is you and Branson Montgomery are engaged."

Whoa! Where did that come from? "Word would be wrong..." I scoff—I literally hate gossip, and to know the workers are prattling on about me and Branson, well it really sticks in my craw. I'm silent as I seethe.

"Come here, Zeta." He pats the lounger, there's only room for one. The anger is gone as I contemplate his sudden invite. Was he testing me to see if I'm available?

Wait.

Is he trying to hook-up with me?

I'm not that kind of woman, but somehow my body takes over, I scoot over to his lounger, and he pulls me into his arms. My body is stiff as it drapes along his, and my heart is quaking—I'm freaking out. I can't believe we're doing this, but what is harder to believe is his effect on me. The arm he has around me is firm, gentle, and his free hand strokes my arm—it's heaven. "Relax...I won't bite. Talk to me." His gentle tone gets into my head and somehow, I feel lighter, calmer.

"About what?" I can't seem to form a thought in my head.

"What are your plans now that you're done college?"

"You're looking at it. I plan on immersing myself in our land by day and stargazing at night."

"That's it?" He sounds surprised. "Not gonna get married, have babies?"

"*Um.* Well, eventually, but I'm only twenty-two. Besides, there's more to living than having babies."

He chuckles in a suggestive way and the mood is gone. I'm suddenly super uncomfortable with where he thinks this might be headed.

"It just got weird. Look, I don't do this sort of thing..." I blurt out, trying to rise and leave. He holds me firm.

"Stay. You know you want to." He doesn't sound cocky, just matter of fact.

"Oh, I *absolutely* want to, but I'm not going to. I'm not looking for a hookup—I'm proudly saving *that* part of myself, until marriage, and I'm uncomfortable with a situation that challenges that vow. Nice meeting you, Nick." I climb off the lounger and start to walk away.

He's in front of me now, blocking my way. He moved so fast, I jump back, startled. He reaches out to touch me, but I shirk it. I'm now wondering what I've gotten myself into—I don't know this guy. I mean he's pretty, but he could be a psycho.

"Don't go like this. I can appreciate a woman who stands up for herself and isn't afraid to speak up. I was only teasing." We both know that he was dead serious, but I allow the apology and nod since I made myself clear. "Listen, I'm supposed to head back tomorrow morning, but I can stretch it until tomorrow night. How about we go stargazing together? I'd love to check it out. I'll find you at your spot, say...just before dark...eight o'clock?"

My head tilts as I consider. Daddy and I can stargaze after—I literally have no reason not to, so I nod again, but I'm still feeling uncomfortable. He sees it and steps aside.

I walk away.

A part of me wishes he'd stop me, and a bigger part of me tells me to turn around and return to his arms, but I don't do it. The fact that for even a fraction of a moment, I am entertaining such a thought is unnerving. I stand by my values, but it still feels like a stretch. I don't hookup, I want more, and I won't settle for anything less, but *oh* how I have to fight myself to remain true.

Chapter Four

The doorbell blaring throughout the house wakes me. Noting it's still dark outside, I panic, wondering what could be wrong as I race down the stairs. I whip open the door to Sheriff Wilkin and his deputy, holding hats in hands.

My heart stops.

Everything stops.

Still groggy, I weigh the possibility that I'm dreaming, but the reality of the officers in front of me snaps me back to earth and kickstarts my heart. What time is it? Why are they here?

The sheriff doesn't show up at the door for social calls at this late hour. My heartrate speeds up, thumping so hard I can hear it. Whatever they're here for cannot be good.

Something is definitely not right, but I'm not sure I want to know what it is.

I gaze back over my shoulder, confused. Mamma and Daddy...They're staying in Mobile. Scenarios play through my mind, affecting my reasoning: their car broke down...that's all...My head swivels, and I search the sheriff's eyes, noting they appear glazy. My head shakes, and I stare off into the space behind them, silently willing the officers not to speak, not to tell me what I'm pretty sure they're going to.

"Miss...Zeta," says Sheriff Wilkin—his voice cracks, but I won't make eye contact, I can't. Instead, I focus on his shiny, middle-aged, balding head, while trying not to faint. "I'm afraid there's been an accident..."

My eyes bulge, refusing to hear it, I blurt out, "They're not..." This time my eyes meet his, searching, praying, desperate.

"I'm so sorry, Zeta. Your daddy didn't make it, and your mamma is in surgery—it—doesn't look good. If you want to change, we'll take you there."

My legs move, and I'm flying up the stairs, sobbing, blind through the hysteria that pours from my eyes. The rest is a blur: getting dressed, leaving the house, the car ride...I'm lost in the dark void of devastation, floating above myself, praying Mamma makes it.

Sitting in the hospital waiting room, I'm told it was a head-on collision. Lydia Montgomery was driving and has passed along with my daddy. Mr. Montgomery is in recovery with minor injuries and Mamma is in surgery—hours pass, maybe it's minutes—I don't know how many as I sit here, stunned, every moment I can ever recall with Daddy passing through my mind.

He's a good man, so kind, supportive, my best friend, the best daddy ever. I'd rather spend my time with him than anyone else in the world—just me and him—working the orchard, stargazing, chatting on the porch at the end of a long day.

I can't believe he's gone, can't accept this cruel reality, don't want to.

It seems so impossible, so surreal. Denial is my crutch, even though I know it's futile.

My fingers coil a lock of my blonde hair around them, over and over, as I think of him—these golden locks, long and smooth, they're not the only trait I got from Daddy. The dirt in my veins, the passion for farming, all the unladylike things that Mamma abhors but also adores about me.

Mamma. My sweet glowing Mamma. She's the only reason I'm not running wild, dirty, and lost amongst the trees. She's the glue that holds our family together. Without Daddy, I'm not sure how we'll survive, how we'll move on. Without Mamma, I'll be alone. No glue, no love, no support.

Swallowing hard, I will away the acid in the back of my throat, forcing myself to be patient, to think positive and have faith, but it's an impossible feat. I've become part of this chair, immobilized by the fear of losing my precious mamma too. I pray, harder and longer than I ever have. I promise God, I beg. I'll do anything if only he'll spare her—she's all I have left.

At some point, I become aware of someone's arms around me. I'm leaning into him, resting my head on his shoulder. Snapping my head up, I search out his eyes.

Branson.

I don't even know when he arrived, didn't even know he was holding me. The second our eyes connect, we both breakdown and sob, clinging to each other for support.

Time passes like a dagger slowly slicing across the flesh when waiting for news on our parents. Branson is able to see his father, but I'm stuck in limbo, sitting in this awful hospital waiting room, crushed by the thoughts about the future that are rolling around in my head.

They play off each other, these thoughts. I have to plan a funeral; my daddy is gone. My mind refuses to entertain the situation with Mamma. She simply has to pull through this.

Branson returns from seeing his dad, and he's ashen, lost, broken.

"How is he?" I ask, worried we might have lost him too.

"He's fine. Only minor cuts and bruises." There's bitterness beneath his words, and he must hear them too because he clears his throat and checks himself. "He was sleeping—I didn't want to wake him."

Nodding, I slouch back into my chair. My butt is sore, and I need to move around, so I rise and start to pace the room, flipping through pamphlets on the wall but not really seeing what any of them are about.

Through the corner of my eye, I sense people entering the room, and I spin towards them. It's a doctor and a nurse, and they don't look happy.

My body jolts as if it's been punched in the gut.

"No," I cry, my head shaking vehemently. "No. I won't hear it. You have to save her!" The air around me thickens, and my vision is blurry, fuzzy. Sucking in huge gulps of air, I try to right myself, but I can't gain control.

The nurse rushes to me, just in time to support me before I collapse, and ushers me to a chair. She sits beside me, holding my hand with one hand while rubbing my back with the other. I'm fighting hard to remain upright as the doctor approaches.

He releases a resolved sigh. "I'm sorry, we did everything we could…"

Nothing else registers, my eyes burn, they're fuzzy—I feel the room fading, everything…fading.

I wake on a gurney, disoriented, the blinding overhead lights burn my eyes. Someone squeezes my hand and my eyes dart to the source as I squint against the invading light.

Branson.

There's a millisecond of confusion, but then everything comes rushing back, and I gasp from the magnitude of my losses.

He reaches out to smooth the hair from my face. "I'm so sorry, Zeta. Your mamma, Constance, was an amazing woman, and your daddy, Russell, he was the father I always wished for..."

Tears fall, soaking my cheeks as I prop myself up on one elbow and reach for Branson with the other. We hold each other, crying.

At some point, I find myself at home, entering our house—a house that will be the emptiest it has ever been. Climbing the stairs, I amble towards the master chambers and collapse onto their bed, hugging their pillows close, inhaling the last of their scents.

In one night, the world around me has crumbled.

It's surreal, but as I lay here spooning their pillows, desperate for a connection to them, I know that this is *all* very real.

They're gone.

Just like that, everything I loved was taken from me.

Gone.

Branson joins me, tucking me in and then crawling in beside me, pulling me into his arms.

How did we get here?

He drove me home. I'm having difficulty recalling much. The only thing I know, the only thoughts forming, revolve around what I have lost and the double funeral I have to plan. These thoughts come in flits, but they're the only ones registering.

Branson holding me in my parent's bed? This doesn't faze me. I need this. I need to be held, and I suspect he feels the same. He's lost too. His beloved mamma is gone, and he is now at his father's mercy. My heart swells with pity and bitterness all at once.

Why would God take three such loving souls and leave the likes of Mr. Montgomery unscathed? How could God be so cruel, so unbelievably unjust?

Why, why why?!

I've never questioned my faith, never doubted, until now. This agony, this pulsing in my chest that feels as though I'm being crushed, brings with it a certain level of resentment, but it's pointless. I know it.

They're gone.

Nothing will bring them back.

God's will. God's plan—I'm sure he has one, but oh how my heart and soul ache—the agony is crushing.

Branson muffles a sob, and it rakes across my heart like a blade. We hold each other tighter, and through our pain and tears we connect in this dark place. At some point, we find ourselves making love—I don't know how it happened, how we both became undressed, but everything seems like it's happening before me but not *to* me—like I'm watching it all unfold, but I'm a willing participant. I cling to him as we kiss and fumble—I'm desperate for something—I don't know what.

My first time with a man and the details I will likely not remember, but I won't forget. I've broken my vow, but I don't have it in me to care. When it's over and he rolls off me, I feel only the agony of loss and regret.

Nothing else.

Maybe in my mind, in his, we thought we'd feel something good when we are both feeling so bad, but I only feel worse.

He pulls me into his arms and within minutes I feel his restful breath on the back of my neck. Sleep won't take me so easily. Loss and shame haunt my every thought. I can't close my eyes. I'm afraid of what I will see.

Crawling out of bed, I dress and leave the house for a late-night stroll. This past twenty-four hours, if it's even been that long, has been the longest of my life and the most devastating.

Lost in heartache, I walk the span of the orchard, taking in the fresh autumn air. Somehow, I make it to our stargazing spot, where the trees stop, and the peanut fields begin. My eyes take in the blanket of stars above me. The sky is clear, and for a minute, I find myself calming, knowing my daddy is here with me, looking down from his and Mamma's place among the stars.

It sinks in. Deep.

They're gone.

It hits me like a hammer in the chest, knocking my feet out from under me. Collapsing to the ground, my fingernails dig into the earth as sobs rack my body to the point that I find myself gasping for air.

I'm alone.

Except, I'm not alone.

Sensing someone in the shadows, my head snaps up. I can't see who it is through the tears, and I'm not sure I care. Continuing my meltdown, I wrap my arms around myself and allow the pain to tear through me as I scream my sorrow up towards the night sky.

I feel masculine arms around me, pulling me up and then cradling me as he lifts me up into his arms. I can't contain any of it, can't catch my breath. Hysteria has a full grip of my sanity. The tears keep flowing, but I stop screaming, I just stare blankly into space as I'm carried through the orchard.

When my body lands softly, I come back to reality. I know by the air around me that I'm in the greenhouse. The cushioned lounger beneath me creaks as I sit up and look around, trying to see through my tears in the dark. Nick sits across from me, concern creasing his forehead as he watches me.

"I'm so sorry, Zeta." The worry in his voice startles me. He *knows*—bad news travels the fastest.

My eyes bulge against the reality of this situation, and my hand flies to my mouth as nausea rolls from my stomach, catapulting what little contents remain up into my throat.

Swallowing hard, I try to defy it, but lean over the edge of the lounger at just the right moment for vomit to spew from my lips. After it's passed, and I sit back up, I notice Nick beside me.

"I'm here if you need to talk about it." The genuine offer tugs at my cold broken heart.

I flinch, knowing I have to say the words—I have to speak the hateful truth.

"It was a car accident...my...parents..." Tears roll down my cheeks, and my throat closes—I can't say anything else—it hurts too much. He yanks me into his arms as I sob, using his shirt as a tissue.

He doesn't speak, probably doesn't have the words—I know I don't. We just sit like this. Time passes, and we find ourselves laying back in the lounger, me snuggled into the nook of his arm as he strokes my back with his free hand.

There's comfort here in Nick's arms, and I feel a sense of calm washing over me. And with the calm comes a quiet resolve.

As if reading my mind, he says, "You'll get through this, Zeta. You'll move on and take care of your daddy's land because he would have wanted you to. You'll live your life, be happy, be strong."

"Yes," I whisper, nodding against his chest.

I will do whatever it takes to ensure that my daddy's legacy continues into the next generation.

Chapter Five

Two funerals in the span of two days: a double for my parents yesterday and one for Lydia Montgomery today. The services pass by as kind words swirl around me, but they're meaningless, like wind passing by my ears. I'm just trying to get through the day.

Since it happened, Branson has been by my side, helping with every detail, supporting me through each day. It's been the longest and most agonizing two weeks of my life of both our lives.

Mr. Montgomery barks orders at his son from across the hall where we gather for tea in memory of Lydia. You'd think the loss of his wife would soften him towards his only son, but it hasn't, not one little bit.

Like a dog beaten into submission, Branson rushes to his daddy's side, intent on doing whatever it takes to make the man happy. Nothing will ever make that man a kinder soul. Just seeing him, just knowing he survived, and my sweet parents didn't—it kills me, and I know, although he's too kind-hearted to say the words, Branson feels the same way.

Within minutes, Branson returns to me, taking my hand and leading me out as the limo arrives to take me home.

"My father has asked me to accompany you home." It's not a question. His tone dictates his need to escape his father.

Nodding, I accept his company, even though I wasn't technically asked if I wanted it. The hour-long ride is silent, just the two of us. We haven't discussed what we did the night after our parents died, nor has he made a move to try again. It shouldn't have happened, and it will *not* happen again. I still can't believe we did it. I gave my virginity to him in a fit of insanity brought on by the deepest sorrow.

"How are you holding up?" I ask, watching him. He's so tightly held together—I can't imagine.

"I'm hanging in there. It's still so hard to believe...to accept." He sucks in a sharp breath to compose himself.

Nodding, I ask the nosiest question of all. "Is your father treating you well?" I know the answer by the slight way he flinches.

"He blames me. Says if they hadn't stopped to drop me off, it wouldn't have happened. He'll take any excuse to make my life miserable..." Bitterness laces his words.

"I'm sorry, Branson. You do know you're not responsible for any of it—it was an accident. What ifs will get us nowhere and only prolong the pain. Believe me, I've had many what if moments."

He breaks down, and I pull him in, consoling him. I feel bad for him; his dad is an awful person. I'm sure under that hard exterior there is some actual love for his only son, but I don't have a clue how to lure it out.

I'm grateful the day is over, that the formalities are over, and I can retreat to my farm.

My farm.

It's all mine now.

This knowledge and all the responsibility that comes along with it, terrifies me. Lord willing, I hope I'm ready for it, but I don't have a choice. The limo drops me off and Branson heads home. As I watch him drive away, my body stiffens—I'll be alone now.

It doesn't last long, though. Workers appear at several points throughout the day, expressing condolences and asking if I need assistance. Before long, I find myself immersed in the everyday tasks associated with farming. It's all a welcome distraction.

For the first time in my life, I made dinner for myself. It was strange only cooking for one, but I couldn't continue eating sandwiches forever. The fried chicken was tasteless, mere sustenance, and nowhere near the caliber of Mamma's chicken. I've eaten and cleared the dishes, but I have no idea what to do now.

That's the problem. The thing about loneliness is that no matter how long you try to avoid it, to keep yourself busy, it manages to creep in. As the sun goes down, I'm sitting on the porch, staring out into the vast pecan orchard. Somehow, I've made it through another day, but I'm restless.

The orchard manager, Clive, should be at his cabin soon, so I make my way towards the workers cabins, determined to talk business with him. Daddy respected Clive enough to share all aspects of business with him, so he and I will work together to continue to ensure my farm thrives.

As I approach the modest white cabin, I notice Clive sitting on the porch, enjoying a beverage. He rises to greet me, sadness painting his handsome features.

I nod, raising my hand to stop him—I can't listen to anymore sympathies. "Clive, I came to talk business, and I just want to do that...OK?"

"Of course, Ms. Reilly. How can I help?"

"Well, there is a lot I know, but the business end has always been with you and Daddy. I guess, I need to know where things stand and then go from there."

"The peanut fields are almost clean, and the pecans are looking fine. We're in for another impeccable harvest. Things run fairly smooth around here. Of course, your attorney James Markham will handle probate and any major contracts and negotiations to our customers. Everything you need to know is housed in the server in the office." He nods his head towards his cabin as an invite to check it out.

"Another time, soon, I'm just about done with today. I appreciate everything you do, Clive. You really are the best manager we've ever seen. Will you meet with me, when you have some time, to show me the ins and outs?"

He nods a thank you. "Of course, I'll be in the office all day tomorrow getting payroll ready to go. Stop by, anytime."

Nodding, I smile and wave as I step away. "See you tomorrow."

I take the long way home, making sure to bring myself to my spot at the farthest edge of the orchard. It's a hike, but the sticky humidity is erased by a slight evening breeze that makes the trek bearable. Night is closing in, and although I should head back to the house, I don't. I just stare out across the peanut fields, taking it all in.

This land is everything to me; It's all I have left of them.

I have to do them proud.

It's my sole focus, my life's breath.

From behind me, I hear someone approaching. Turning, I see Nick's silhouette moving towards me. I haven't seen him since the night he picked me up off the ground in this very spot and consoled me, because he had to go back to college.

Tilting my head with surprise, I smile, happy that he took time out of his weekend to visit me. His presence is suddenly everything I never knew I needed.

"Good evening, Zeta," he says, his tone gentle, low, and incredibly formal.

Swallowing hard, I collect myself and smile. I don't think I've smiled in ages. It feels weird but seeing him makes me happy, genuinely. "You drove all that way just to be here...I appreciate it," I say.

"I'm sorry I didn't call first, but I wanted to see you." He grins and my heart lurches in my chest. "I'm sorry I didn't make it to the funeral. I had an exam."

"It's okay, for all I know you were there—the whole day is a blur." Sighing, I try to stop the tears that are ever present. "Nick, I never got the chance to thank you...for picking me up off the ground that night..."

He steps closer, his face inches from mine, and tilts his head to the side as if he's assessing me. "No thank you is necessary. You needed me."

Oh boy, did I ever. *Do* I ever. I don't know what to say that won't come off as bonkers. My attraction to this man is intense, crazy, and when he's near, my dreary world brightens.

He's my worker, he and I shouldn't—but he isn't my worker, not anymore—still, would it be wrong? As if reading my jumbled thoughts and protesting them, he reaches out, pulls me into his arms, and takes my lips. My feet stumble, my hands move up to brace myself and the palms rest against his chest and then fist the material of his shirt, holding on.

His soft lips tease mine as a low rumble rises from within, pushing a soft moan of pleasure from my lips. It's needy, surprising me, so I pull from his lips and turn to rest my head against his shoulders. The comfort I feel is overwhelming and I know that in his arms, my soul is safe; I'm not alone. He kisses my head and holds me. Enough time passes that I start to feel awkward, lost, confused—this is too much—far too much too soon and I suddenly feel like a caged animal.

I pull back, searching the space behind him for an escape. I want to flee—run in any direction, but at the same time, as my fingers loosen their grasp of his shirt, I'm sure of my want to cling to him and never let go. Suddenly, I want more—all of it.

Panic sets in.

I can't do this.

It's bad enough that I tossed away my promise to save myself for marriage and slept with Branson on a whim of despair, but I can't just sleep with someone I hardly know. I have to nurture some sort of value—start fresh, although, it's not like I'm getting my virginity back.

What would my parents say?

Like a second bucket of ice water has been splashed in my face, my body twitches as I stumble back from Nick. It's not because I don't want him. I do, and the realization that I can do what I want, unprotested, *that* is the hardest to take.

Again, as with everything else I do, I'm reminded, they are gone.

Nick reaches out for me, but I shake my head as tears start. "I can't do this...I..."

"Don't," he says, reaching up to thumb a tear from my cheek as his other hand reaches for mine. "I understand."

"No," I say, sighing, feeling deflated. "It's just too much." I really like him. I don't understand how or why, but the attraction is out of this world. It's just a really bad time. I'm not even slightly ready for anything.

"Listen," he says, still holding my hand. "I'm heading back tomorrow. We'll keep in touch, OK?"

The thought of him leaving me is more than I can bear. Like a giant baby, I start to cry, sobbing as he pulls me against his chest. What's wrong with me? How can he even want me when every time he sees me, I fall apart?

It's better this way, if he leaves, and we get to know each other. Besides I need space and time to figure out my life, to grieve, to heal.

Space and time, I'll be alone in that space and time.
Lonely.

Being alone and being lonely are two totally different feelings. I used to welcome being alone—I lived for it—now I dread it because loneliness takes over.

Loneliness: It's a black hole of nothingness and the most unbearable feeling of all.

I want to go home. I want to crawl into my bed, pull the covers over myself, and just sleep my pain away.

Defeated, I turn to leave, and he doesn't stop me. As my hand slides away from his, agony returns with each step I take. It's a feeling in the pit of my stomach that tells me this is the last time I will see Nick.

It stops me. I can't lose any more. I have to tell him how I feel, even if I'm not exactly sure what that feeling means.

Spinning, I search the space, but he's gone as if I imagined the entire exchange.

Chapter Six

One foot in front of the other. That's what Pastor Rogers says will get me through the days. It's literally how I'm coping—my feet are moving, my body is moving, despite my broken heart.

I'm officially alone and can't stand the thought. Sure, I have my workers and the odd acquaintance, but it's not the same. Somehow, I have to navigate this life, this booming business that Daddy created, and not blow it.

I'm terrified. I'm so lost, so...*Ugh*.

Ugh.

That *ugh* feeling that pretty much sums up the whole of my existence.

Getting out of bed this morning was torture, but I did it because of this moment: standing in the yard, watching Nick pull up in his car. My body aches with trepidation. I can't say goodbye to him, I don't have it in me. I move towards his car but halt, frozen, because he emerges from the driver's side with a wrinkled red ball of fur in his arms.

Tears pour from my eyes as I break down. Before I know it, Nick is hugging me as close as he can get with the floppy-eared puppy between us. This is the last time I will feel the comfort of this man's arms around me.

Pulling away, he kisses my forehead while handing off the puppy to me. I hold it close, nuzzling his chubby face as he licks me relentlessly.

"Old Man Carson saved him just for you. I hope you don't mind—I hear redbone coonhounds are a lot of work, but I figured you needed him. Mr. Carson will be stopping by soon with his papers and supplies—you won't have to worry about anything, just take care of him, and he'll take care of you until I get back."

"Thank you, he's perfect." I'm trying to be polite but am elated by his words—he intends to come back.

He reaches out and takes my free hand, pulling me back into his arms. "I hate leaving you, but I have to go. I'll be back to visit you at Thanksgiving, and we'll call or text every day."

My head nods against his chest. "I'll miss you." I'm not sure why I said it, I hardly know him, but at the same time can't imagine not knowing him. It's a strange and giddy feeling and it lifts me up. He cared enough to bring me a puppy, to make sure I had someone to keep me company. In this moment, even though I have no idea what to do with a coonhound, I'm so grateful for the sentiment.

He's still holding me when he says, "What are you going to call him?"

I hesitate for a second, but then the name comes to me. "Rigel, for Orion's brightest star."

"Of course," he chuckles. "Next time I see you, we'll finally go stargazing together. Promise?" I nod against him, happy to think about next time.

At some point, we pry apart, and he leaves.

Now, here I sit, on the porch, unable to motivate myself to move but mostly I can't imagine putting this adorable little cuddle machine down. It was the most thoughtful gift anyone has ever given me and something I had no idea I needed.

The sound of a vehicle coming towards the house captures my attention and I realize it is Mr. Carson. He skids to a stop and hops out of the pickup with surprising agility for a man in his seventies. Reaching up he removes his hat and nods a hello as he approaches.

"Mr. Carson," I say, nodding a greeting.

"Hope you don't mind me popping by without calling first, but Nick assured me you'd be waiting." His impeccable Southern manners make me smile.

"It's more than fine. Thank you for parting with one of your prized pups. I am so grateful," I say.

"He's the last of the last of the best," he says, grinning as he reaches out to scratch the snoozing puppy on the head.

"Oh?" I say, surprised by his statement. Mr. Carson is the most well-known breeder of coonhounds in probably the world. I know this little lad is of good stock.

"Other than my Ellie and Rodney, I'm getting out of the breeding game, starting to think about retiring..."

This grabs my immediate attention. Mr. Carson's land aligns mine. If he sells, I want—my Daddy would have jumped hoops for a shot at the Carson land.

"Are you thinking about selling?"

"Yes, ma'am. Probably not until Spring, but I'm getting too old and tired."

"Well, you could have fooled me the way you jumped out of that pickup."

He chuckles, nodding his head towards the pickup as an invite for me to follow.

As excited as I am about the puppy, I'm focused in on that little tidbit of intel he slid my way. "Mr. Carson, please, don't list—if and when you want to sell, I want it and will give you fair price for it. You know, my daddy always had eyes on your land."

He spins, eyeing me with such intense sadness. "Again, I'm so sorry for all you've lost—that's more than any one person should have to bear." I vaguely recall his sentiments on the day of the funeral, but I acknowledge his words with a nod. "Russell was a decent man. I'd surely sell it to you and not look back, but how are you going to manage all this *and* that?" He waves his hand through the air—I know it's a lot, overwhelmingly so.

I straighten, determined to make my point. "I'm going to manage it the same as my daddy did—this land is my everything. It's all I have left of them, and I am determined to make it thrive."

He chuckles, shaking his head as if recalling a memory. "You're so much like your daddy, and so full of spunk."

"Thank you." I am like my daddy and proud to be so.

"And now you have a hound on your hands...I hope you know the trouble they can get into." He's teasing, but also serious. I've heard tales my whole life, but I don't care—Rigel was a gift, so he and I are gold.

I shrug and grin. "I got this."

"I believe you. Well, I'll take him off your hands for training in a few weeks. Your beau paid for and arranged everything. He's mighty fond of you, that one."

My cheeks flush, but Mr. Carson busies himself unloading all the supplies for Rigel from his pickup, so he doesn't notice my schoolgirl reaction. Knowing Nick did all this for me, warms my soul. By the time we've unloaded and set everything up in the house, I'm done.

The emotional ups and downs of the day have gotten the best of me, but it's my mind that is causing me the unrest. It's swirling with hopes and dreams, Nick, Rigel, and the Carson land, I would *love* to acquire.

It's a lot to take in on any given day, but for me it's sucked up my last drop of energy. I feed Rigel, take him outside for a short walk, and then we head to bed. Snuggling in with my wrinkly little lovebug is all I need to drift off.

Chapter Seven

Nick's been gone for thirty-three days. He's texted daily, checking in, and we talk on the phone every other day or so. We've bonded over shared pictures and stories of Rigel and the everyday orchard business. The more I get to know Nick, the more I miss him.

Being alone is the hardest part of everyday. Getting out of bed for no one is agony. It's a job that each morning I force myself to do, and it's because Nick gave me Rigel. Knowing he needs caring for keeps me moving.

But it's more than Rigel, it's the thoughtfulness of all of it. Our conversations last for hours, and we chat about anything and everything, and he doesn't patronize me in any way—he's become my best friend—I look forward to sharing everything with him.

I have Rigel to quell the loneliness. He's kept me busy, but he's a joy to have around. His bouncy puppy energy is the reason I get out of bed each day. Because of Nick, breathing is bearable, living isn't a death sentence—I'm excited about the future.

Until yesterday, I lived on it—simply seeing his words pop up on my phone made my day. Finding out I'm pregnant with another man's baby erased all that. At first, I thought my missed period was due to stress, but a quick trip to the CVS and several tests later confirms it.

I'm pregnant.

Phone in hand, I sit on the edge of my bed in tears, lost, scared, happy, excited, all at once. The second I knew I was pregnant, a huge weight lifted—like I now know I won't be alone. But the man I'd rather be the father isn't, and the man that is the father is on his way over. I haven't told Branson, but I know he'll be supportive.

In my heart, I know he'll be a great father too. His dad treats him so poorly, that he'll do whatever it takes to separate himself from him.

Where will Nick fit into all this?

My grip on the phone tightens. I can't bring myself to call him. I know it will mean the end of whatever it is we started. My heart aches with that knowledge, and I don't think I can take it.

I want Nick, I think I might be in love with him. He won't have me now. What man would?

The doorbell chimes, causing me to jump. How long have I been sitting here lost in thought? Surely, Branson isn't here, already. I move to the window and see his car parked outside. My stomach drops.

Since my parents passed, I seem to have no regard for time.

Moving to greet him, I open the front door, and he smiles while yanking me into a hug. We haven't seen each other in weeks, since the funeral. I've avoided him at all costs, but now I can't keep hiding.

Wrapping my arms around him, I try to gage some sort of feeling but there isn't anything but friendship. Pulling back, I nod towards the sitting room, welcoming him into my home.

"How have you been, Zeta?" His regard is genuine, as always, he's cordial, kind, and the space between us is relaxed.

My legs take me to the sofa, and I sit—my thoughts are chaos—I'm basically a zombie, a zombie that has no idea what to say. Staring ahead, a moment passes as I try to find the words, but then the only word that matters flies from my lips. "Pregnant." Swallowing, I close my eyes while he plops himself down beside me.

He's silent for a beat, stunned, but then he recovers and nudges me. "Marry me?"

My eyes bulge, connecting to his as I laugh, surprised, but not really. "What? No...I..."

"Come on, Zeta. It makes sense. Your parents wanted it, my parents wanted it—fate has stepped in. We're going to have a baby." Excited, he looks around and waves a hand in the air. "You need help. You can't do this all on your own. I can help, be a husband, a father to our child."

In his words, he omitted *us* wanting to get married, and I really don't want to marry him. Branson's a good guy. I've always known it, but I've also always known that I don't and never will love him. Even in this moment, I feel nothing but friendship for him. I suppose it's better than nothing, but I can't just marry him.

He's not Nick.

He leans in and kisses me, soft, tender, hopeful. Still, I feel nothing. Straight-faced and unmoved, I inch away and eye him. "We discussed this...before...Branson, we're not in love...You know as well as I do that when we...it was a mistake...and you'd be committing to a life with me when maybe there's someone else out there for you...and I want..."

He cuts me off before I can say Nick's name. "I'll care for our family like any man would. I won't want anything else, and I still firmly believe love will grow. We get on well, don't we?"

"Yes, but..."

"Look, I know this is a lot. You don't have to answer right now...Just think about it and let me know." A huge smile curves his handsome mouth, and his eyes light up. "I can't believe I'm going to be a father. This is...well it's just the best thing to happen to me in forever. No matter what you decide, I'm with you, one-hundred-percent."

In a daze, I show him out, promising to be in touch. The phone is still in my hand. I have to do this, I don't want to, but I have to, and I'm not doing it via text like a spineless coward.

I dial his number and wait.

He picks up. "Hey, baby. How are you?" The cheer in his tone cuts deep.

Again, the word just pops out. "Pregnant."

He's silent, obviously shocked, knowing it can't possibly be his while wondering about all of it because on the night we met, I was adamant I was saving myself for marriage—I feel sick. I should have told him what happened. I was hoping to forget about it, but a lie of omission is still a lie.

"It's Branson's baby." A tear slips from my eye, burning a path down my cheek. "After my parents died...we...it was a stupid mistake...but we did it..." His silence breaks me. Knowing I've hurt him is tearing me up, but honesty is my only option. Seconds pass and I wonder if he hung up. "Are you still there?"

"What am I supposed to do with this, Zeta?" He sounds...like he's trying to compose himself. No doubt, he's angry. In my deluded daydreams, my thoughts about how this would go down, I hoped he'd accept it, that we would move on. His tone tells me I *was* delusional.

With everything else going on, everything that I've lost, the thought of him shunning me is too much—I can't hear it, I won't. "I just thought you should know. Branson asked me to marry him." The second I say it, I snap my mouth shut, regretting it. The coldness and spite in my words—that's not like me. I've given him no opportunity to come to terms with this. What is my problem? *Ugh*. Squeezing my eyes shut, I wait for what I know is coming.

"You two should be very happy together," he says, his tone tight, like he's clearly trying to keep his cool. There's a moment of silence, followed by a sardonic huff. "Take care, Zeta."

Before I can say anything more, he disconnects the call. Staring at the screen of my phone, I'm stunned, absolutely gutted. I blew that whole conversation in the most pathetically epic way.

He hates me now.

I shouldn't have told him about the proposal. Now he thinks I'm into Branson. The one person I had hoped would support me will likely never speak to me again.

Did I really think it could have gone better?

Yes.

Maybe he'll come around. It's just a shock. Thoughts of him coming to me and sweeping me into his arms, telling me we'll be together no matter what, that he'll love this baby, they swirl through my mind like perfect fiction.

Fiction is *not* my reality.

But to just hang up, to just leave me hanging when I'm so in love with him it actually hurts. Choking on a sob, my chest constricts. I've lost him.

Who can blame him?

Well, if he can just walk away, if he can just cut me off like that, then I guess I was wrong about him. Anger, and shame, and complete humiliation, rage through me like an emotional rollercoaster moving at lightspeed.

It isn't meant to be. Those words twirl through my mind as I mope up to bed and crawl in. It's five in the afternoon and I'm in bed, exhausted, done, and that feeling of utter despair once again takes control.

Lying here, staring at the ceiling, one thought comes back to me. My mamma would be over the moon to hear Branson and I are having a baby. She'd insist I marry him. So maybe I just should.

Mamma was so sure we'd grow to love each other, that we'd make a good match.

"Branson," I whisper, but his name doesn't stir a single sentiment of desire. But I don't loathe him. He's not disgusting, he's kinda hot in a handsome prep-school kind of way. And he's a good person, supportive. He would never just hang up on me like...Nick's face comes rolling into mind, and it's the last thing I see in my mind's eye as my eyelids close.

Chapter Eight

Clearly, I never make the best decisions where Branson and I are concerned. It's like I don't know how to say no. It's sad, pathetic, and usually ends up with me on the losing end.

Although, is it really losing? I mean I am gaining a beautiful child, and...a husband. It's not conventional, but it's happening.

When we told Mr. Montgomery about the baby, he was furious. He went off on a tirade, belittling his son in front of me as if he was filth. That provoked the pity feels, and like a dimwit, I blurted out that Branson and I were in love and getting married as soon as possible.

At the time, I just wanted him to stop yelling because he was freaking me out. He did, and just like that, he smiled and gave his son a friendly congratulatory pat on the back. And just like that, I said yes to Branson, even though I wasn't going to say yes to Branson.

I never imagined my wedding would take place in our backyard, performed by a justice of the peace. Mr. Montgomery insisted we marry as quickly as possible, the only thing holding us up was the unavailability of the pastor, so here we are, getting married in the most impersonal way, by a stranger, shotgun style, except Daddy isn't here to wield the weapon.

I always pictured my daddy giving me away, in a church, with our local pastor and congregation all gathered to celebrate. Today those dreams are far away. Pointless.

The ceremony is a blur.

The entire day is a blur.

I'm hot, sweating in my pink sundress as I feign happiness.

It's surreal, and I have to keep reminding myself that I married Branson, that we're going to be parents.

My hand rests over my tummy as I silently assure myself, for the hundredth time, that this is right. Our baby deserves two parents that will love it, and we will, without a doubt.

I wish my groom was Nick.

I wish my parents were here.

I wish my mamma was here to help me through the day, to offer advice, to hug me.

I really could use a hug. I'm terrified. What if Branson and I don't make a go of this? What if we don't grow to love each other and instead grow to despise each other?

I prayed, I pray, that isn't the case.

I actually *do* want to be happy.

It's possible. I need to believe it to be so.

Arms encircle me from behind, and Branson leans in to kiss my neck. He's happy about this. I'm trying, but all I can think of is Nick, even though he hasn't spoken to me since the phone call, one-week-ago.

Before I knew it, the wedding was happening, and I was too ashamed to try to smooth things over with Nick—if I'm honest, I've been a spineless fool, and I know it. But it's an impossible situation and I had to, *have* to, let him go.

We're over.

It sucks, my soul aches with it, but it's reality.

Branson and our baby are my future, so from this moment on, I will focus on them and better days.

"Let's go to bed, Mrs. Reilly," Branson huffs into my neck. My stomach flips, hearing him refer to me like that—it's what he called my mother. It's creepy. Maybe keeping my maiden name is a mistake. No. It's all I have left of them, it stays.

Taking my hand, he leads the way as I follow him upstairs to consummate our marriage. When we cross the threshold to the master bedroom, he pulls me into his arms, kissing me with such passion that I almost feel something. But it feels robotic, a role I'm playing, and one I will continue to play until hopefully one day it doesn't feel rehearsed.

When it's over, we curl up together, and I lie awake while Branson doses. My thoughts are chaotic, my current situation seems so surreal, and not what I imagined, so I'm feeling emotional, fragile, jaded, but one thing soothes me. My hand rests on my tummy, silently telling my darling baby that I love it and will do anything for it.

I wake to find the bed beside me empty. Glancing at the clock, I see it's five in the morning. True to his word, Branson has taken off and running, determined to manage the farm. His keen business sense means he can focus on the numbers, and I can dig in, working the land and greenhouse. Hands on is my preference anyway.

He must have run off to meet with Clive. I know there is much to be discussed. A smile finds itself on my face. Not a big one, but an almost contented one. Branson is a man of his word, and he will take care of us. This I know.

We're safe. And even if Branson and I don't make a go of this marriage, my land is safe, thanks to the iron-clad pre-nup I had James draw up. No matter what, I have to take care of my family's legacy.

For the first time in weeks, a sense of positive light washes over me. Sometimes things don't work out exactly how we picture them, but that doesn't mean they can't be awesome.

It's time to start living.

It's time to start planning, for our family.

I can't wait to hold our baby, to gaze into its eyes, to love it, and watch it grow.

Nick's face jumps to mind, but as usual I push it out of the way. He didn't want us. He chose to walk away, and I have to respect that. At least, he didn't fill me full of lies and promises—just honesty—the burning kind.

Branson has only ever been up front and honest. And yeah, neither of us are under any illusions about the other. We're just husband and wife and friends who happen to be having a baby together. With time, I think I could love him, and I'll have a partner, a husband, a *family*—I won't be alone, ever again.

Whimpering catches my attention, and I move to peek over the edge of the bed. Rigel's puppy eyes gaze up at me expectantly. My heart melts and I move to lift him onto the bed for a snuggle. It doesn't last long, he's too darn hyper, so I crawl out of bed and prepare to start the day.

Chapter Nine

For marrying a man, I wasn't in love with, I have to say that I'm reasonably content—resolved. Branson is a wonderful husband. He's been attentive and committed to making Reilly Farms thrive. Each night as we gather for dinner to chat about our day, I am more comfortable with our arrangement.

His interest in the farm is more than I could have hoped for, and I've grown to respect his business sense. He's jumped in, working side by side with Clive, ensuring harvest is a success.

I know it will be.

Tonight, I'm seated on our chaise on the balcony outside the master bedroom. The heat has been bothering me the past few days, so I've stayed inside and rested. Pregnancy fatigue is crazy, I could literally pass out comfortably on a bed of nails. And the nausea—*morning* sickness—it's more like anytime sickness and it's relentless, but I'm coping.

"How are you feeling?" Branson asks as he joins me, offering a glass of ice water.

"Tired, but good." Smiling, I take the glass and sip.

"Come. Let's get you to bed." His concern and willingness to take care of us is sweet, and I'm grateful for my husband's friendship.

Nodding, I rise from my seat, but then the room starts to spin. Before I fall, Branson has me and guides me towards the bed.

"Maybe you should see a doctor. It can't be normal to be dizzy," he says, the shaky concern in his voice is evident.

As swiftly as it arrived, the dizziness is gone. "I feel better now. My pregnancy guide says many women suffer from the odd dizzy spell, but I'll call the doctor tomorrow." Snuggling into bed, I'm relieved the second my head hits the pillow. Branson crawls in beside me and pulls me into little spoon position.

In the dark, when he holds me, all sorts of thoughts run through my head. A part of me believes it is possible that we could make this marriage work, that we can be happy.

The past few weeks have been better than I imagined, and Branson has been a support I didn't know I needed but am thankful to have. I find myself excited to be a mother, excited for the entire journey, and thankful that Branson is here beside me.

Is it possible that with time, I could fall in love with my husband?

I think it might be.

MY EYELIDS FLUTTER open to stark white lights and people scurrying all around me. Dazed, I try to focus, but I feel strange and so weak, like I'm floating away from myself. It's peaceful, inviting—the frantic noise around me muffles as I close my eyes and drift.

As if waking from a nightmare, my eyes pop open and search my surroundings. The beep of machines and bedrail tell me instantly where I am, but confusion as to how I got here rushes through me, bringing on instant panic. Trying to move gets me nowhere, I feel like a heavy rock is holding me down, and I can't muster the strength to sit up.

"Hey there," Branson's familiar voice coos as he leans in to look me in the eye—his are red, like he's been crying.

My heart drops. That familiar lump of loss has returned with a vengeance, squashing me beneath its weight.

Sometimes you just know things. Like at this moment, I read the agony in my husband's eyes, and I know it's my own. Tears fall as my eyes leave his to search the air, trying to recall how it happened. How did I get here? How did I lose my baby?

"What..." I say, my voice dry, crackly. My throat aches, and I can't get the words out—they're too painful.

Leaning away, Branson returns with a cup of water and straw and puts the straw to my mouth. Drawing back the cold liquid, I try not to choke, but my throat is raw, and I'm so depleted that the simple action of sucking on a straw is stealing my last drop of strength. Confusion doesn't help.

I was fine.

We were fine.

Branson takes my hand as tears fall from his eyes. "When I woke up this morning you were unresponsive and lying in a pool of blood. You hemorrhaged; they weren't able to save..." He chokes on the last words, turning away as sobs shake his body. My bed quakes from the magnitude.

The questions I have are many, but they're muffled by the deep knotted ache in my chest that is clogging my throat.

My baby.

Tears soak my cheeks, but my anguish is silent—shock prevents the words, buries the questions—none of which really matter, anyway.

My baby, my hope for the future, my heart...It's gone. All is lost and in this exact moment, I wonder what sort of cruel God would make me endure this heartache—*more* heartache—I've had enough, and it seems impossible that I could survive this.

I want to scream, lose it, but I don't have the energy.

I'm done, done with life, done with *everything*. Turning my head, I stare to the side of the room opposite Branson, avoiding his gaze, but mostly unable to stomach his presence.

This is wrong. Why is everything worth anything taken from me? Do I not deserve a little happiness, *something?*

Eleven weeks ago, my life spun upside down, but I was finally at peace with it, I was happy about the future.

Eleven weeks.

It doesn't sound like a long time, but it feels like eternity.

I remember reading in my pregnancy guide: most miscarriages happen in the first trimester. We were so close. My poor little angel is with my parents now.

And I am still here.

With nothing.

I gave up the man I wanted to marry the father of my baby, and now like some sick cruel joke, my baby is gone, stolen from me.

My baby is *gone.*

Gone...

I'm never going to hold my baby, never going to look into its eyes—I so looked forward to becoming a mother, to...all of it.

Like a dam, the torment erupts, and I bawl, hysterically and uncontrollably. I feel Branson leaning in, holding me, but it means nothing. I can't stop, and I'm having a hard time catching my breath.

Through my tears, I see a nurse fiddle with my IV and within seconds, I calm, float, soar away from my pain. The hysteria stops, and I welcome the sweet oblivion that unconsciousness offers me.

I hope I never wake up.

What's the point?

Chapter Ten

Six months later.

"Well so much for that." Looking towards the gray afternoon sky, I curse myself for this latest foolish predicament.

This morning when I woke up, I had an overwhelming urge to work—to actually get my hands dirty. I've spent too long wallowing, neglecting my birthright. My plan to spend the day tending seedlings in the greenhouse made sense, but I became sidetracked along the way.

The workers were hedging and knowing that there were hundreds of trees that needed it, I had to lend a hand. But then I got out the ladder—I shouldn't have gotten out the ladder. Moving from tree to tree and climbing a ladder to really inspect the branches is one of my favorite things. Unfortunately, it's a world I become lost in.

So stupid...

Gazing out across the peanut fields that border the Carson property, I note the nastiness moving in. There's calmness in the air, quiet, the kind that precedes the opening of the sky before a storm. It literally lasts a second or two and then water shoots from the clouds like someone dumped a giant bucket from the sky.

I leap from the ladder, ducking beneath the pecan tree. What a joke. The tree's lush leaves are no match for the torrential downpour that mercilessly soaks everything in sight.

Sputtering from the monsoon invading my mouth, I accept my drenched fate.

In Alabama, you can never count on the weather. I know this. Everyone does. The weather can change with the blink of an eye, and if rain is in the forecast, it's usually torrential or flash flood material. Hell, I'm lucky there isn't a tornado heading my way.

I should have been paying attention to it, should have noticed the black clouds rolling in, but I became engrossed in my work—lost among the leaves, oblivious to the world around me.

So stupid...

It's difficult to see through the sheet of water pouring down, but as I glance around, I notice the workers have left, taking the hedgers and vehicles with them. I swear they were here, just minutes ago. Weren't they? Even Rigel ditched me.

How long was I up there?

I can't believe they left me stranded.

No. I *can* believe it.

Gritting my chattering teeth, I scoff in disgust. "Of course, they left me behind—they're probably laughing it up back in their cabins." They have no respect for woman, but one working her *own* fields, garners less respect.

Before I married Branson, I never had a problem. I know it's hypocritical for me to judge them as I myself have fallen victim to old school social conventions—my marriage will never be anything other than a business transaction.

Something changed in me when I lost our baby. Something changed in our marriage, and although we married in haste because I was pregnant, we haven't recovered from the loss.

Branson is still there for the farm, tirelessly ensuring everything moves along—he took care of everything while I sunk into the deep pit of depression.

It took me six months to claw my way out of the dark, but while I was lost in grief, things changed. I don't know why, and I don't know how, and worst of all, I don't know how to regain their respect, but I'm not going down without a fight. If I survive this storm, I'm going to raise holy hell with my disrespectful workers.

Women of my position don't get their hands dirty. It's simply unheard of. Even though times have changed, old school mentality remains cleverly veiled behind the guise of progression. Still, this marriage is about as regressed as I will ever be. No way will I play the role of obedient wife and homemaker. This is *my* land, *my* orchard, my *home.* Generations of Reilly women have loved and worked this land, determined to make it flourish, and I will continue the tradition.

I'll work these trees and soil until my fingers bleed if it means ensuring they thrive.

I will *not* lose any more.

Standing here, whining and cursing, isn't going to get me out of the storm. The nearest shelter would be my house, so I guess, I'm just going to have to walk in this nightmare.

I inch out into the open, trying to assess what is coming. Rain burns my eyes, pelting my cheeks with force. The storm clouds appear to stretch for miles with no immediate end in sight. This storm has just gotten started and won't relent anytime soon.

Taking off, I sprint, dodging under each tree along the way in hopes that they will provide some shelter from the rain that is slapping against my skin.

A tumultuous crack of thunder rumbles through the sky. My body jolts, and I squeal as a bolt of lightning zips past my head, striking the next tree in my path, less than ten feet away.

Stunned, I stop running and stand frozen, gaping at the giant pecan tree that had been split in two and now sizzles as the rain drowns out the fire. Just like that, one of my most productive trees, and one of the oldest is destroyed.

That could have been me.

Another crack of thunder startles me back to attention. Screaming, I race for cover in a zigzag pattern, not really sure where to go or what to do but praying to Jesus that I don't get fried on my way back to the house.

With each thunderous bang, my eyes scan the sky, mesmerized yet terrified by the sheet lightning sailing across the sky in every direction. If I don't find shelter, I'm going to get fried. Another bolt passes overhead, and I snap, screaming as my body shuts down. Fear grips my senses, forcing me to crouch into a ball, covering my head with my arms—as if that would save me, but I'm literally too petrified to move.

Huddled on the ground and trembling with fear, my mind races to come up with a plan that doesn't involve me getting zapped, but with each crack of thunder I shrink that much more into myself—all reason is gone.

If I survive this, it will be a miracle.

How could I have been so stupid, careless?

I might actually die today, get fried into oblivion. I really don't want to die, not yet. For the first time in a long time, I *don't* want to die. I *want* to live. Oh, what a perfect time to have such a revelation.

Suddenly an arm rounds my shoulders, encouraging me to stand while forcing me to run. Looking up, I catch the eyes of Nick. Stunned, I swipe the water from my eyes, unsure of what I am seeing. He drags me along, my feet stumbling while trying to keep up with his pace.

"This way!" Nick's voice is barely audible over the raucous of thunder and rain. He holds me against him, guiding me to a pickup parked off to the side.

Overjoyed with gratitude, I whip open the door and climb into the passenger seat. Breathless, I force myself to recover as Nick jumps in, fires up the pickup, and starts towards the main house.

Turning to him, I eye him, and it must look as though I'm questioning my sanity because he throws me a couple of looks, like *he* thinks I'm insane—I think I might be, some days.

"I was out making sure my men had taken cover when I saw you running," he says, focusing on the road. "What the devil were you doing *that* far out from shelter by yourself?" It wasn't a question, more like a comedic observation. I can laugh now, I suppose, but this man's sudden presence forbids it.

I'm not sure this is real. Did I get zapped? It's like I've entered an alternate reality.

The awkwardness of it forces me to babble—anything to avoid the larger question. "I know it was stupid, I got side-tracked on the way to the greenhouse and then...I don't know...I just...lost track of time..." Shaking my head, the question blaring between us bursts from my lips. "What are you doing here?"

"I guess, you didn't know." He sounds surprised by my question, but I really have no idea what he's referring to. "I've been working for Old Man Carson, helping him get his property in order before the sale—there's still seeding to take care of—I thought Branson would have mentioned all this—I've been promised a job here, as Clive's assistant, once the sale goes through."

Wait. What? He's been hired to work here? How can Nick want to work for me after what passed or didn't pass between us?

He probably just needed a job. It's his dream and in this economy, you gotta take what you can get...Still, it's awkward. He could go to any number of orchards. My stomach twirls with hope—did he come back for me?

I'm married, and he knows it.

Like a caged animal, I start to fidget, contemplating an escape, but I don't like my chances out there. Trying to act casual, I nod and stare out the window.

Branson and Clive take care of the business end of things. It's not hard to imagine I didn't see Nick around—I haven't been on the Carson property in months. I've been lost, distracted, and trapped within the hard walls of grief. I've only recently started leaving the house and involving myself in the business again. Branson's taken care of everything, and he and Clive do all the hiring. They wouldn't know about my history with Nick—I never said a word.

This can't be happening. I've accepted my losses and have been trying to move on. Nick's presence is welcome and unwelcome all at once. I'm not sure I can handle it.

Nick slows down, trying to see through the windshield. The wipers are useless against the thick stream of water. "We have to stop for a few minutes. I can't see a thing."

My head nods, but the words won't come out for fear they'll be followed by tears. If Nick hadn't come by...I...

Ugh.

Nick sits silent as I rant inside my head. He must think I'm beyond ridiculous. Despite the rain, the air inside the truck thickens; it's stuffy and beyond awkward, but at the same time, it's absolutely freezing. My drenched body trembles, my teeth chatter. The AC in the cab blasts my flesh—the trembling and chattering intensify to the point of convulsion.

Nick reaches behind the seat and retrieves a blanket, passing it to me. It's warm, not having been chilled from the AC. Wrapping it around my body, I snuggle in, grateful for him, once again. I shouldn't *be* grateful. Not really. I want to scream and yell and tantrum.

None of this is funny. None of this is fair.

"Mrs. Reilly." Nick clears his throat. "Don't take this the wrong way, but why do you putter about the orchard like a farmhand?"

I gape at him, stunned: A, that he called me *Mrs.* Reilly, and B, that he literally just said that. "*What?*" I scoff, glaring at him with disbelief. "This *land* is my father's legacy—I need to know it's being looked after."

"You have workers...and Branson." There's a hint of something in his words: spite, bitterness?

"I love this land and the feel of its red earth beneath my fingernails—you *know* this. Besides, I feel bad when I see the others working hard, when I can easily lend a hand... Sitting around while everyone else does the work drives me nuts."

"Yes, but pruning trees? The hands are paid to do the grunt work. You don't have to, and it ain't safe for a woman..." He stops and grins, knowing he sounds ridiculous, I'm sure.

My eyes blink rapidly, not believing that he just went there. *Ain't safe for a woman.*

He grins, nodding as if chiding himself. "I didn't mean it to sound like that...well, you don't have to is all."

Chewing the inside of my lip, I seethe, frustrated with the same old stereotype and still miffed with my workers for bailing on me. I'm not about to put up with any more crap today, that's for sure. "Since when did you become sexist? I'm kind of embarrassed for you, right now."

Nick laughs, shaking his head. "It doesn't matter any to me what you do, but I know the other workers have a problem with it...I hear them talking..." He abruptly stops himself. "Sorry, that wasn't fair."

"I know what people say—my own *husband* says the same, but I don't care. I love working my land, and I will continue to do so until the day I die." I stick my nose slightly in the air, defiant and pleased as punch that I got the husband-dig in, because quite frankly he's making madder than a wet hen. No one will *ever* dictate to me what I should and shouldn't do with *my* land, and I can't believe we're even having this conversation. He *knows* this about me—it's as if he's forgotten—and *that* knocks the wind out of me.

Nick chuckles. "Well, okay then. It looks to be calming down a bit out there. Let's try to get you home, to your *husband."* Ouch. I want to vomit, lay down on the ground and die. That literally felt like a knife to my heart.

The playful way he says it sends chills down my spine. It's been months since our short-lived and barely acquaintance, but I remember his arms around me, his kiss. I remember longing for him. I remember the final phone call.

"I thought you hated me." It blasts from my lips before I can stop myself. But it must be said—we can't just pretend that nothing passed between us.

He's silent for a beat and then sighs. "I did at first, but then...I know you did what you had to do."

"Why come back? Why *here?*" My question comes off as snippy, but I'm confused by all of this.

"Well, I finished college, and I need to work...so...Old Man Carson laid the offer on the table before I returned to school." He's grinning, and it's cheeky.

"You know what I mean, Nick."

He sobers. "You're a happily married woman, now. What we had—well, it's ancient history."

It doesn't feel so ancient and hearing him refer to what was the most fulfilling time in my life, until it went to hell, *as* ancient history, makes me kind of want to cry. Ancient history—I'm dying on the inside.

Lost in thought, I can't find the words to continue this conversation. I want to tell him everything, but I don't like saying the words. Even now, after all this time, it's like a knife across my heart. He's right, I'm married, and that's that.

By the time we reach the main house, the rain has slowed considerably but is still pouring. Turning to Nick, I place a hand on his arm, surprised by the heat of his flesh. A familiar tingle flashes through my body, followed by a rush of heat that I pray isn't blushing my cheeks. Nick turns to meet my gaze; our eyes remain locked for several silent seconds.

Feeling slightly unnerved by him, I mask my reaction by plastering a fake smile on my face and casually switching the direction of my gaze.

"Thank you." My eyes meet his again, and I smile, releasing a short giggle. "If you hadn't rescued me, I would have been fried. Really, I owe you one."

"No worries at all, ma'am." Nick nods goodbye as a casual grin curls his lips.

My skin crawls.

Ma'am?

I hate that word, I'm far too young to be addressed with it. Too much has passed between us for *him* to address me so courteously.

But he will soon be my employee, so...

Tearing my gaze from his, my hand swipes across his arm as I remove it from his flesh, but the caress causes another rush of excitement to pass through me. My heart quickens and suddenly, the words are lost to me.

What is wrong with me?

I need to get out of this truck.

ASAP.

Before I flail myself at him like a flaming torpedo of desire.

In a flash, I wrench the door open, toss it shut, and race up the stairs to the porch where Rigel sits, waiting. He's obviously much smarter than his mistress because by the looks of him, he's bone dry.

Chapter Eleven

If I had started to dry off in the truck, it's impossible to tell because I'm soaked all over again. By the time I enter the house, I'm a shivering mess of wet clothes, dirt, and utter confusion.

Stopping in the vestibule, off the front entryway, I strip out of the clothes that have become a second skin and lean against the wall trying to absorb what just happened.

Nick's back, and so is his effect on me. I thought I was over him. I most certainly never expected to see him again.

Convulsive shivering disrupts my chaotic thoughts, forcing my eyes to scan the vicinity for something to cover my naked body. There's nothing tangible in sight, so I go in search of a hot shower, and dry clothes.

I've showered and dressed and here I stand, staring at the floor—the magnitude of Nick emotions course through me. I'm near tears, fighting hard to not break down. I'm not sure I can handle him being here, not sure my heart can take not being with him. And I won't be with him. I'm no cheater, nor am I a quitter—I committed to a marriage with Branson.

The phone rings, snapping me out of my funk, and I race to grab it. "Hello," I say, out of breath.

"Zeta, it's James." His all-business tone tells me something is wrong. "We have a problem—*You* have a monumental problem."

"*Oh?* What's going on?" I can't imagine a reason for James to call sounding so serious, unless...

"Ballentine got wind of the deal and they've countered your offer plus twenty-percent."

My heart stops and I feel sick. Ballentine is my only real competitor, they're already twice my size. "*Twenty* percent? Wait. How did they find out we were bidding on it? Mr. Carson wasn't planning on listing it."

"Exactly. How *did* they find out?" James says, his voice cooing, suggestive of something sinister. "Obviously, *someone* in your employ spilled the beans."

"James, the only people who knew of this acquisition are you, me, Branson, and Clive. Are you suggesting...?"

"Yes, Zeta. Do the math." His blunt condescension irks me.

"Well, it doesn't matter. I fully trust our management. Clive has been with us for years—he wouldn't dare, and Branson...Was it you?" I know it wasn't, but he's vexed me, so this is what he gets.

He laughs, knowing it's a dig. "How do you want to proceed?"

"I'll contact Mr. Carson myself. Surely, he'll listen to reason. He's been a neighbor to our family for years, and he respected my father, they were friends. I'm sure, he'll tell Ballentine to take a hike."

"I wouldn't be so sure, Zeta. Money talks. Can you afford to counter?"

"I'm not sure. I'll speak to Clive and Branson and get back to you."

"Don't dally."

We hang up, and I plop onto the mattress of my bed and toss my phone at the pillow. I want Carson's land. I need it. This has been in the works for months. If I don't get it, Ballentine will grow even bigger. And I don't like the idea of their land being up alongside mine.

Edward Ballentine is as relentless as he is fierce. He could care less that the land may connect to mine. He just wants to drown us out.

I need that land!

Reaching for the phone, I dial Mr. Carson.

"Mrs. Reilly, how nice to hear from you." The smile to his tone tells me he was expecting my call.

"Mr. Carson, you can't sell to Ballentine. My daddy wanted that land, *I* want the land. Do you really want it to become the property of Edward Ballentine?"

"Listen, Mrs. Reilly. Times are tough. I can't do this anymore, and the offer is such that I can retire comfortably."

"Whatever they offered you, I'll match it, and you can stay in your house. Please Mr. Carson." I'm not too proud to beg—I'll do whatever it takes.

He sighs on the other end. "Well, all right. If you pay what they offered, I'll take it from you. I'd surely like to stay in my home. You've always been a sweet girl, and I have no interest in playing you off each other. I just want to retire and get out of the confounded business once and for all."

"Thank you. I'll have James amend the deal, and we'll make it happen, ASAP."

"Of course. We'll chat soon, dear."

A long-relieved sigh blows from my lips as I hang up the phone and fall back against the mattress. Thank god, James warned me. I don't know how he found out, but I'm grateful for his slippery lawyer dealings. He seems to be the eyes and ears I need.

I wonder who leaked it to Ballentine. It wouldn't have been me or Branson.

Wait.

Lifting myself up, I walk over to the window and stare into space. If Ballentine offered such a chunk to acquire that land, he'd drop a pile more just to drown me out.

My stomach flips, and my head shakes vehemently—I don't want to entertain the idea.

A new thought takes hold, and its deviousness takes my breath away. Nick just happens to work for Carson and soon to be me. *He* knew about the deal. Given our history, is it possible he's the rat?

Maybe he's not over what went down between us.

Maybe he's out for revenge.

Fire burns to my cheeks as fury takes over. It had to be him. *Well!*

We'll just see about that. I'll not have Nick working here—not when he's so clearly trying to ruin me.

Noting that the rain has finally stopped, I finish dressing and race out the door, hop into my pickup, and head straight for Clive's cabin. On the drive over, I calm considerably. In my soul, I don't believe Nick would be the rat. He could have left me to fry in the storm, but he didn't. If you want to destroy someone, you don't rescue them from dying. There was a time that I knew him—he wouldn't do something so underhanded. I *know* it.

I shouldn't let James get in my head.

Ballantine's counteroffer is moot. Mr. Carson is selling to me. The color drains from my cheeks as I realize how much money I committed to this deal. It wasn't going to be a stretch before meeting Ballantine's offer because I have significant savings thanks to the life insurance money. What if it's too much?

Clive and Branson will know what to do. I'm sure we could afford it, but I need to know we can *manage* it. I don't want to leave us short in case of an emergency. They'll be at his cabin doing paperwork, like they often do during rainy weather.

I pull up to park a few cabins over because the front of Clive's is under water, and I don't want to get stuck. Thankful, that I wore my boots, I slop my way through the massive puddle to the front porch. I pull me feet from my boots and walk barefoot to the door.

From inside the cabin, I hear Clive call out. Startled and concerned, I open the door but halt in the doorway as if hitting a brick wall.

The sight before me is...

I'm not seeing it.

No way.

Rapidly blinking while trying to convince myself that what I'm seeing isn't real, I reach a shaky hand up and brace it against the door frame. More moans fill the air, burning my ears and flushing my cheeks. My grip on the door frame tightens as I struggle to hold myself upright.

What the...

Am I *really* seeing this?

Gaping at the scene before me, I nod confirmation. Clive and Branson are kissing and writhing around naked in Clive's bed—it's passionate, it's...*Oh my God!*

Swallowing hard, fighting the bile rising in my throat, I try to make sense of the scene before me and my swirling thoughts. My cheeks burn hotter, my vision becomes fuzzy—I try to steady myself, but the world goes black.

My eyes open to fully clothed Clive and Branson standing over me and muttering, back and forth, but I can't hear their words. My eyes skip from one man to another while nightmarish images flood my mind, reminding me of what the two of them had done—what they'd *been* doing—for how long?

Shaking my head vehemently, I try to deny the reality of which I'm now faced, but it can't be done.

My husband, Branson, has a gay lover. Branson is gay?

In a thousand years, this isn't something I would have ever suspected or expected. Branson's dwindling affection for me hasn't been a surprise given what we've been through, but he still attentive, cordial, and...obviously just playing the part.

And, all the talk about starting a family.

I never for a second thought he had taken a lover—never in my wildest twisted dreams did I imagine his professional relationship with Clive had morphed into something more. But it has. I see it in their mutual exchanges of concern and fear and...*love?*

It's definitely love.

Am I dreaming? I mean this entire day has been one big nightmare. Now more than ever, I'm convinced I got zapped by lightning.

Branson and Clive.

Branson and *CLIVE!*

As I sit here, I realize it might not be *that* big of a shock, and it certainly explains a lot—like his long working hours with Clive. And we never have connected on a physical level.

There is only so much one could take, and I think I've reached the maximum limit. I might have been able to continue with this loveless marriage, *if* I hadn't seen what I did, but that kind of thing can never be unseen or forgotten.

My throat clenches. I'm barely able to speak, but somehow the words croak from my lips. "I gotta get out of here." I need to be alone. I need to process. Between Nick showing up, and the land deal, and this—I can't handle *this*—it's just too much.

Honestly, all I ever wanted was a quiet life, working my land, watching the stars...This sideshow that has become my normal is bonkers and absolutely unwelcome.

Branson leans over me, covering me with a blanket as he blatantly ignores my panic and helps me up and over to the bed. Clive stands back by the door, watching, unsure of what to do or say.

"Zeta." Branson kneels beside the bed and takes my hand in his own. "I'm sorry you had to find out this way. I never intended to hurt you."

A snort escapes followed by sarcastic laughter. "Oh, come on, Branson. You and I both know that *this* isn't a real marriage. I'm stunned, to say the very least, but I guarantee you that my feelings are most definitely *not* hurt."

Taken aback, a brown tendril of Branson's hair falls across his forehead. He brushes it aside and rakes his hand through his hair, his handsome face stressed from the strain of worry.

He rises and sits on the bed, next to me, leaning his head against mine.

My heart hurts for him, for us. We've both lost so much and have gotten everything so horribly wrong. Still, I value his friendship and am thankful for what he's done for me, for my father's land.

"What are you going to tell your daddy?" I say, shaking my head.

Mr. Montgomery is about as old school as a man of the South could get. He will most definitely not take kindly to the revelation that his only son is gay. As if my husband didn't have a bad enough relationship with his daddy.

The pity feels take hold, and I shudder to think what his daddy will say to him. I can't even imagine, but for the first time in months, I don't actually care. Their twisted father-son relationship is no longer my problem. Branson shakes as sobs rack his body. I place a consoling hand on his leg and pat it while he breaks down.

Sure, technically, Branson cheated on me, but I'm not upset, not even a little. I feel…light…like a huge weight has been lifted, and I can *finally*, really and truly breathe.

Clive steps forward and places a hand on Branson's shoulder. "It's time, Branson. We can't keep on like this."

I rise to leave, forgetting all about my original purpose for visiting Clive. It doesn't matter because I'm buying that land. I'll sell my soul to make it happen.

Still lost for words, I leave the cabin, slide back into my boots, and amble towards my pickup. My world has once again flipped upside down, and I'm not really sure how to make it right.

The door to the cabin closes, and I turn to the sound, looking over my shoulder as a smile curves my lips. One wonderfully exciting option, swirls through my mind—the immediate end to this sham of a marriage.

Chapter Twelve

Yesterday was insane. The emotional rollercoaster feels like a dream, like it all happened to someone else. I'm awake, snuggling with Rigel, having slept the sleep of angels in my Bransonless bed.

I'm finally going to be free, and the idea makes me giggle with anticipation. Leaping from bed, I take care of Rigel, shower and dress, intent on getting a head start on the day's work. I need to stay ahead of the game, especially now that I'm acquiring more land.

It's after nine when I make my way through the orchard and notice there aren't any workers about, and the strangeness of it has me concerned. I don't even see my dog, and he's never far away. It's eerie—something is off. Changing direction, I head to Clive's cabin intent on discussing the land purchase.

A reminder of yesterday's debacle stops me cold.

Ugh!

How is this going to play out now that he and Branson are together? I can't go back to the cabin. I'm not ready to face either of them. Pulling my phone from my pocket, I frown, not sure what to do.

I text James. *Deal back on—get it done!*

The awkwardness of finding Clive and Branson together is enough to make me change direction again. My train of thought is scattered—I close my eyes, forcing myself to focus.

Three key needs play across my mind—my checklist of tasks to get done ASAP: One, discuss the pending Carson acquisition; This is priority one. Two, reprimand the workers that ditched me in the orchard yesterday; I can't let that slide. Three, figure out just where Clive and Branson fit into all this now that...

Sweet baby Jesus—my life is a mess!

"Mrs. Reilly." Nick's voice calls out from behind me. My eyes pop open with surprise, and I swing as he approaches, eyeing him with suspicion. Rigel is with him and sits at his side once he stops. That's one mystery solved. Little traitor.

"What are you doing here?" I snap, not meaning to sound grumpy, but I'm beyond anxious.

"Carson sent me over. He knew Ballantine was about to strike." He pauses, and I can tell he's struggling with what he needs to say.

"Well, go on then," I say, urging him to tell me what he knows.

He sucks in a sharp breath and on exhale, he says, "Clive walked, and he's taken the majority of your workers with him."

"*What?!*" The surprise in my tone comes out more like a screech. "Wh...Where..." My mouth snaps shut. I can't even say a word—I don't want anyone knowing what I walked in on yesterday.

"Edward Ballantine picked him up this morning..." He looks away as I gape at him, stunned. He clears his throat awkwardly. "Branson went with them, and from what I hear, Ballantine made an offer to snag your workers too."

"Oh my God!" That snake in the grass lost his bid on Carson's land, so he did the only thing he could to ensure my ruin. Nodding, I spin, prepared to storm off but I stop. Where will I go? I haven't got any cards left to play. I drop to the ground, done, defeated, not even sure what to do or think. "What am I going to do?" The question falls from my lips with a pitiful huff, not really to Nick in particular, but more so for the universe.

I can't believe Clive went to work for Ballantine, but honestly, it's not like he could continue working here, not after yesterday. I was a fool to think he'd stay. Not that I really thought he would, but in the cold reality of today—this is a complete disaster.

"Clive was the best there is...I *trusted* him...and my workers...How could they just leave? I'm about to purchase scads of land...I need them." Tears start to fall, and breathing feels tight—I hyperventilate, leaning forward and placing my face in hands. I try to regroup but I'm losing it. Rigel nudges me, licking my hands as if trying to cheer me up.

Nick crouches down in front of me. "It will be ok, Mrs. Reilly." Him calling me that doesn't help. I snort out a sardonic laugh.

"Really, Nick?" My eyes swing to his. "How?"

"Let me take over. We'll use Carson's workers while I fill the vacancies—they would have been yours anyway...I'll have the vacancies filled before you know it." His offer is more of a command, but since I'm up the river without a paddle, I'll take it.

My eyes light up. "You'd do that for me? Yes! *Please!* We have so much to do, I can't be without a full crew."

"If I do this...I want Clive's title," he says, and he's serious, even if it is an awkward request.

"I don't know..." The look on his face freaks me out. He's willing to help, and right about now, I'm in no position to bargain. "Yes, just...Nick, if you can get my farm running and keep it above water, then you can have Clive's title. I'll do just about anything." He's already got his phone in hand and is dialing. He reaches out, offering me a hand and I take it, letting him hoist me up.

Sweeping my hands over my butt and legs, I clear the dirt from my clothes and straighten up. He nods to me, letting me know he's got this, and I turn and walk towards the cabins to clean and prepare them for new hires.

Clive left me with six workers. Six! Trying to stay positive, I recall my list and how it really isn't a problem anymore. I'm buying that land. Edward Ballentine can go straight to the devil for all I care. And he can have Clive, and Branson, *and* my disrespectful workers too.

As I move from cabin to cabin, assessing the state of affairs, I pray to God that Nick comes through for me—I also thank God, over and over, that Carson and Nick have my back. This all could have been worse. Now, it's like a massive housecleaning which is actually what I needed.

The majority of the cabins have been cleared out and not left in the best condition. I'm too stressed to deal with the mess. I drive back to the house to grab supplies. When I pull in, James is just getting out of his car.

As I get out of the car, I raise a hand to stop him. He didn't even call first, which is beyond rude, and I'm in no mood for more bad news. "Don't even speak unless the deal has been made."

He laughs, throwing back his head. "It's as good as done. Did you find out who the mole is?"

There's that—I now wonder if Clive was the mole, but then again it could have been any one of my rogue workers—I'm learning that they gossip worse than my mammas old church group. Sighing, I shake my head, looking away. "I'm sure it doesn't really matter, now."

"Right. Well, now that Clive is working for Ballentine, we can only interpret his role in all of this...*and* Branson..." He stops himself. It amazes me how much he knows. My eyes search his, wondering if he knows the rest. He arches a cocky eyebrow. Yup. He knows. Great.

Smiling, trying to make light of my situation, I say, "I wonder, do you do divorces?"

He laughs again, shaking his head as he plops his briefcase on to the hood of his car. "I did your pre-nup, so of course, I'll handle it—my usual fee."

The one thing I adore about James is his ruthlessness as a lawyer and his inability to care what the case is. He's in it for the money: pure and simple.

"Now, what are you going to do about a manager? I've got distributer contracts that need signing, and we need to discuss permits and...I suppose you could..."

I raise my hand to stop him. "Nick Harper is my new manager."

"Nick Harper?" he drawls with question. "How did you find someone so fast?'

"Well, he's Carson's field man and was to be Clive's assistant once the deal finalized. He's the logical choice and has stepped up." I sigh, throwing my hands up.

Taken aback, he shifts his footing, eyeing me. "Hold on. You hired a field hand to manage? Zeta, as your lawyer, I have to tell you..."

"Never mind, I know what I'm doing. He's not just some field hand, he's educated with a firm interest in management, *and* he knows the land."

"Interest. Right. Well, you know best. Where can I find this...Nick?"

"Right here," Nick says, strolling up to us. "What can I do for you?"

James turns, holding out his hand to Nick—they shake as James introduces himself. There is a snide trill to his voice as he announces, "I'm the Reilly family attorney. I handle all the contracts, legal affairs. You and I have some things to discuss."

I cut in. "Nick, you go ahead and talk business with James. I need to prepare the cabins for the new hires. Call if you need me." Leaving them, I stroll into the house, stopping just inside the door to peek through the window and watch their exchange.

Nick seems serious about this role. I'm not sure how I feel about it, but I'm also sure I have no other option. There is no way I can manage a farm of this size on my own, and I won't go down without a fight. It's just a matter of checking off the things I need done and moving on to the next item.

Picking up my phone, I call Merry Maids be Mopping to come and deal with the cabins—mostly I don't want the job—especially cleaning the Managers cottage where my husband took his lover. My body shudders against the image of the two of them together. It's something I'm probably never going to forget, although I sure hope I can.

By mid-afternoon, I find myself fully operational. The maids have finished and vehicles containing new hires and their belongings have been arriving at a steady rate since noon.

My husband and his lover are gone from the picture as if they were never really there.

The chaos of the last twenty-four ridiculous hours has waned and life is moving on. Raising my face to the sky, I silently thank God, again, for sending Nick back into my life. If he wasn't here to take over, I don't actually have a clue what I would have done. It amazes me how he always seems to be here to pick me up off the ground.

Chapter Thirteen

Two Months Later

Reclining in my chaise on the balcony, outside the master bedroom, I sip my mint julep while casually observing Nick hard at work. His presence affects me, but it's always professional. The problem is my memory—it's like an elephant and recalls every detail, conversation, moment, as if replaying it on a video screen in my mind. Too many heated moments have passed between us, and it's starting to feel like we will never cross the professional barrier into something more.

And I *do* want more.

I crave his electric touch like a junky craves heroine.

Nick is my heroine, and that drug has made getting out of bed in the morning possible.

A satisfied grin curls my lips as my eyes rest on Nick and as usual, I'm amazed. He takes pride in his new position as orchard manager and ensures that all the workers are well-trained and looked after. At the moment, he's standing with Juan, our new hire, under a pecan tree several feet away. Rigel sits next to Nick as he and Juan chat. They look to be involved in an intense conversation, seemingly oblivious to my stalker gaze and Rigel's adoration. My almost grown puppy spends most of his day trailing Nick, but at night he's home with me.

Tearing my eyes away, I watch the bustle of workers as they wrap up for the day, happily heading home to their cabins at the far eastern edge of the pecan orchard. All of the cabins are full, thanks to Nick; he even hired a field manager to run the peanut production. He runs a tight ship, but the workers respect him and are content with their positions. The best part is that these new hires treat me with respect, they're not a bunch of traitors like my last crew.

The orchard has never run so smoothly and the acquisition of the Carson land, which could have been so stressful, was a piece of cake. The new land aligns with our peanut fields and will triple the size of our peanut crop. Two hundred pecan seedlings have been planted along the edge of the fields, creating the perfect framework for a flourishing business. If this keeps up, we might surpass Ballentine's production within the next ten years.

Looking down, I stare glumly at the divorce papers on my lap. I couldn't be less interested in reading them but have forced myself to skim the pages. Everything looks to be in order, but the legal mumbo-jumbo bores me to no end. Giving up, I sigh, drop the papers, and stare up at the setting sky.

A lot has happened in the past two months, but time raced by with a blink of the eye.

Branson and I haven't talked in weeks, but I learned that he and Clive had been together since shortly after my miscarriage. I was completely oblivious. I owe it to the fact that I was miserable and just ambling through life—through our marriage.

Although he was furious at first, Mr. Montgomery came around and has started speaking to his son again, but it's still a sore subject. Those close to the couple know the truth about their relationship, but to the rest of the world, Branson took a position with Ballantine after his marriage to me fell apart.

No one dares speak the truth out loud because as much as being gay in the South is still, very much, the worst taboo in some circles, crossing Mr. Montgomery is worse. In fact, by order of Mr. Montgomery, a *Defamation of Character* clause had been negotiated into the divorce contract.

My lips are forever sealed on the matter. We're both free. Neither of us could ask for anything more. Branson is happy, and I'm getting there.

The farm flourishes, and I've escaped the binds of a marriage that should never have happened. My eyes water when I think of the losses, of my parents, my baby. By the mercy of all that is holy, Branson and I have been given a second chance, a chance to make better decisions and to have what we truly desire.

A resolved sigh escapes my lips as I scan the orchard. My freedom is a double-edged sword—I'm alone again, *lonely*, sometimes to the point of desperation. Now that Branson's gone, I have no one to talk to—I still miss his companionship.

I have Rigel, thank goodness. His devotion is something to be admired, but still...

My gaze levitates back to Nick. The remembrance of that rainy night, of his arms around me when my world came crashing down, brings immediate heat to my body, reminding me of just how lonely I am.

Nick is not an option for me. Since his return, he has only been professional. Without saying a word, he's made it clear that his interest in me is strictly business. If I thought losing

Clive was bad, losing Nick as manager would ruin me—in more ways than one.

Strictly business.

I have to respect that.

Besides, I'm through with making bad and often impetuous choices. So, I'll remember the moments we shared, but it's time to move on.

I want a man who can be with me. I want to experience real love with a man who loves me as much as I love him. Living on a farm, in the middle of Nowhere-Alabama, doesn't exactly increase my chances of finding that man.

Pulling my attention back to the divorce papers, I read on. The farm has been in the Reilly family for generations and is safe in the divorce thanks to an airtight pre-nup—James made sure it was protected.

Each of us leaves the marriage with whatever we came in with. Had the Carson acquisition happened while we were together, we would have split the ownership, but given the circumstances, Branson has decided not to make an issue of it. It was my family's money that paid for it, anyway, so I keep sole ownership of the farm. The rest are details that don't much matter to me. Soon, I'll meet with James to sign the final papers, and our sham of a marriage will finally be behind us.

Looking back on our marriage, now, it all seems so far away—like it didn't even happen. It shouldn't have happened, but I am thankful for the opportunity to move one. I certainly don't miss Branson. Not really. But I miss having someone who cared for me, even if it was all a part he was playing. I'm more positive than ever that he saw me as a means of escape from his daddy and I am more than understanding on that front.

I miss my parents, I long for them, every single day. I'm so desperately lonely. How disappointed would Daddy be in my trail of bad choices since their tragic passing? I miss spending time with him, puttering around the farm or stargazing. Those nights spent gazing upon the heavens with my favorite person will never be forgotten. It's those loving memories that get me through the tough moments.

Returning my attention skyward, I close my eyes, welcoming the last bit of sun on my face before it sets for the night. The slight breeze cools the air, making the otherwise dank humidity tolerable, and the fresh scent of magnolias in bloom invades my senses. It's calming, Mamma always smelled of magnolias.

I need a hug. I need *something*.

I'm going stargazing. I need to. Finding the time to stargaze is a challenge because the farm keeps me busy. It's either too hot or too rainy and the right balance can be difficult to find, but tonight is about as perfect as it can be.

Taking advantage of the clear night sky, means I'll have to endure the sticky heat, but it will decrease as the temperature drops as it does most nights in early summer. At the moment, conditions are ideal and one of few opportunities to view Orion at its finest without having to endure the unscrupulous heat of a typical summer evening.

My eyes wander back to Nick, and his eyes meet mine as he nods a good night and then he and his new recruit stroll towards the cabins. Watching him walk away hits me in the chest—I love having him nearby. It soothes me, makes me feel safe, but he's also a distraction. Checking myself, I snap out of it and wander into the bedroom.

Crouching beside the bed, I reach under and retrieve my leather telescope case and plop it down on the mattress. A smile crosses my lips as my fingers caress the brass tube of my antique telescope, admiring the slick cool surface. The change in temperature could sometimes fog the lenses, so I leave the case open, enabling the contents to acclimate as I prepare for the journey ahead.

Dressed in a pink, cotton, sleeveless, maxi-dress, I pull my hair into a ponytail. Eyeing my reflection before heading out seems silly since I'll be alone, but I do it anyway, out of habit, because a lady always makes herself presentable before leaving her quarters. Mamma taught me that and enforced it without question. Staring into my own brown eyes—the one feature inherited from my mamma—my heart feels heavy with the pain of losing her.

I need this tonight. I need to be closer to Daddy, to Mamma, and stargazing is just the thing to do it. It's as close as I can get anyway.

The reflection in the mirror shows the darkening sky behind me, so I snap out of it and prepare my gear. Giddy with anticipation, I toss a blanket and water bottle into my backpack, grab a folding chair and the leather case, and race down the stairs and out into the night.

Rigel, who was waiting for me on the porch, bounces along beside me for the half-mile walk to my usual spot on the northern edge of the pecan orchard. It's a hike that could be done blindfolded because I've walked the path a thousand times. I always walk it, taking a car deprives me of the magic. Watching the sky transform from shades of pink and orange to purple and blood red, before the blackness takes over, always amazes me.

The progressing sunset lights the path for most of the hike, and then the moon and burst of stars between the trees take over, providing enough light for the remaining trek. The moment I move past the last of trees and into the open peanut field, my whole world changes. It's like bursting out of a dark box and into Heaven's light.

Hauling my gear through the southern humidity is a guaranteed workout, but I love every minute of it, even though it leaves me drenched in sweat. Dropping the gear, I stretch my arms above my head while scanning the evening sky. Orion shines brightly, and the stars of his belt glisten, demanding attention.

A night like this makes living secluded from civilization worth it.

Months of loneliness, being trapped in a marriage I never really wanted was only tolerable because I had this—my escape. Time spent with grandpa's telescope, cleansed my soul and eased the burden of grief, even if just slightly. Gazing up at the stars, reminds me of Daddy—I'm closer to him on nights like this—it's as close to a hug as I'm going to get.

Since Branson's departure from my life, I've busied myself with the running of the orchard, leaving little time for socialization. Pecans and peanuts are my livelihood and the brilliant evening sky my only company.

Each time I peer through the eyepiece of my antique telescope, I think of Daddy. I miss him so much.

After taking a refreshing swig of water, I set up my chair, mount, and telescope, and then lean into the eyepiece.

Overwhelmed with excitement, I focus in on Orion's belt. Oh, how I love that constellation and the science behind its stars, but mostly Orion represents a connection to my beloved Daddy and in these moments with my eye to the sky, I'm with family.

Blissfully engrossed in the vibrant vision that is the Orion nebula, I take no notice in planet Earth until a shadow moves in front of my field of view. Startled, I shriek and jump back.

Chapter Fourteen

As my eyes adjust to the change in light, the intruder's face comes into focus, and a sigh of relief blows from somewhere deep within. Recognition of the man before me registers, and the fear that became relief morphs into irritation.

"Nick! You scared me to death. What do you want?" I don't know why I snapped at him and instantly feel bad. "I'm sorry. I didn't mean to snap at you."

"I'm sorry I startled you, *ma'am*, but it's hard to avoid in the dark. I was out walking the orchard and noticed you watching the sky...Can I have a look? I've never had the opportunity to see the stars through a telescope before." Nick's dark eyes glow with excitement.

I'm stuck on the word *ma'am* and am still more than annoyed with his formality towards me—it feels so wrong and completely out of place, especially given the fact that he's standing before me, shirtless, in all his muscular glory. I mean...

"Nick," I say, barely able to hide my irritation. "I've told you so many times—please, don't call me ma'am. It makes me feel...old."

"Sorry, Mrs. Reilly." His formality makes my heart hurt.

"That's...worse." I cringe, closing my eyes. "Zeta, *please*..."

Nick chuckles, and I realize he's just been playing. "Zeta, may I?" He nods eagerly towards the telescope.

"Of course." Stepping back, I invite him to move in. Memories of the night from hell come flooding back to me as I recall how we had made a date to stargaze all those months ago, the night my world came crashing down. The ache in my heart intensifies and tears well up. Sniffing, I focus hard on pulling my emotions into check but then I just start babbling, like I often do in the presence of this man. "It's focused perfectly on Orion's nebula, which is actually a cluster of stars and gases. When you look up at the sky, it looks as though there is only one star, but a strong enough telescope reveals the truth."

Nick comes around and leans into the eyepiece. His muscular arms flex from the movement, and the moonlight reflects off the flesh of his sweat-dampened back, highlighting his divinely chiseled torso. Sucking in a sharp breath, I avert my gaze and try to clear my head. It can't be done.

Biting my bottom lip, I clench my fists so tight my nails dig into my palms. I'm fighting a silent battle and desperate urge to reach out and touch him, with every fiber of my being. I know it's wrong and I promised myself that I would be true to my vow of abstinence before marriage. This time, I won't stray, but being in Nick's presence really tests my self-restraint.

Closing my eyes, I pray to Jesus for strength, and it helps. The cobwebs clear and I can breathe, although my heart is still thumping around in my chest.

I open my eyes and force them to change direction and gaze upon Orion. As glorious as the stars in the sky are, I can't clear the awkwardness of Nick's nearness from my mind.

I shouldn't have invited him to gaze because I'm right back where I shouldn't be—pining for my employee.

"Wow. I can't believe the colors," Nick says, stepping back and staring at the sky with admiration. "Do you mind if we change direction? I'd love to look at Betelgeuse."

Taken aback, I raise a brow, impressed. "Lean in to look and guide your hand around the dials, like this." I focus on demonstrating, welcoming the diversion. "This one will change the power and the other will focus. It's an old but powerful telescope."

Nick leans in and focuses on changing views, while I step back, hoping the darkness will cloak my emotions—I'm sure it radiates all around me like a flashing neon sign that reads: *I still want you.*

This is as close as I've been to Nick, in a non-professional manner, since the night he rescued me in the rain. Before the moment that passed between us, before he came back into my life, I thought I was over him.

I think I was wrong.

Actually, I was definitely wrong.

I'm *so* not over him, not even close, but there is a clear line here, and we shouldn't cross it. He's my employee—and good managers are hard to come by—without him, my farm would be in ruin. I can't broach these feelings with him because since he returned to my employ, we've only ever discussed the farm, and that's exactly how it should be.

Now, here he stands, sharing something deeply personal with me while I ogle him. It's unsettling, and definitely perverse, but I'm at a loss as to how to stop myself. My nerves are beyond frazzled.

Unsure of how to handle these increasing desires, words fall from me like a rambling fool as if speaking will somehow drown this fire burning through my veins. "My daddy named me after the third star in Orion's belt, Zeta Orionis, also known as Alnitak...It's actually a cluster of three stars. I think that's why I am so drawn to it. I don't think I've ever seen anything as beautiful."

"I have," Nick says as he turns, locking his eyes on mine.

What?

Gobsmacked, words are lost, but I hold his gaze—the intensity sears through to my core. Snapping my gaping jaw shut, I smile lightly, trying not to outwardly swoon. It's bad manners not to acknowledge an accolade, but I can't get past the awkwardness between us, and if my instincts are correct, it's entirely mutual.

Nick looks towards the sky, his expression changes as though he's scolding himself.

"I best be getting on." He clears his throat. "Tomorrow comes early." Catching my gaze, for only a second, he nods goodbye, and ambles off, leaving me speechless.

Loneliness swoops in, swirling around me as if locking me within the walls of a tightly held prison. A prison that's suffocating me, testing my sanity, and it increases with each step he takes.

Asking him to stay would be bonkers and incredibly impetuous.

"Please don't go." The words blow from somewhere deep and needy. Did I really just say that out loud?

Nick stops in his path and turns slowly to face me as if *he* can't believe I said that. We stare at each other for a moment before desperation takes over, forcing my legs to move in his direction. Something beyond my control pushes me towards him. Nick makes no move as I approach, but when I throw myself at him, crashing my lips to his, he pulls me into the warmth of his embrace.

He returns the kiss, brushing his lips against mine in a soft and unpresumptuous manner. My insides are bursting with anticipation, with the need for this and so much more. I hold on tighter, needing him to know my heart but it back-fires. His body goes rigid. He pulls away and looks into my eyes, but it isn't passion that burns me with his gaze, it's sadness.

"This isn't right, Zeta. I can't be this way for you. You deserve more than I can give you." Nick means the words, it's there in the agony behind his tone.

Hurt morphs into anger. Turning away from him, I cross my arms, feeling exposed, vulnerable. The yo-yo of emotions fires me up, causing me to swing back in his direction, ready for a fight.

The sullen look in his eyes softens my pending rage, but I still need to make a point. "You know, social status and position don't mean anything, not really, not...This is stupid—we're still attracted to each other—it's not one-sided... I want to be with *you!*"

Nick shakes his head, looking awkwardly away.

An invisible line separates us, and it's a line that I probably shouldn't cross even though I really want to. His silence tells me he doesn't feel the same. I read it wrong. His effect on me has turned me into a mindless fool. I back away, turning my gaze skyward while staring sadly up at Orion as a tear escapes my eye. "I want to feel like a woman—be loved like a woman—the way being near you makes me feel."

Nick remains silent and makes no move behind me. It's not his fault that I find myself lonely, and my *situation* is not his problem. I know my behavior is out of line, but oh how I want to feel alive for one moment in time. Expecting him to be the cure for my loneliness is ridiculous, but I wish for it anyway.

"I'm sorry, Nick." I smile lightly, trying to mask my disappointment, but my tone is laden with sadness. "I'm just so lonely...I wasn't thinking. I'm sorry. I shouldn't have thrown myself at you...Please go. We won't speak of this again."

Nick still doesn't speak, but I hear him walk away.

Cursing my overactive hormones, I plop myself down in the chair, lean my head back, and stare at the sky. Nick's a bigger gentleman than I'd like him to be. What happened to the guy who made it very clear he wanted a hookup in my greenhouse? Oh yeah. I got pregnant and married another man. I drew *that* line.

This entire situation is of my own creation. Maybe the reason I want him is because I'm stuck in the past, hanging on to the what ifs, and there are so many what ifs...

But what we had is over. I have to accept that and move on. Maybe I should go into the city once in a while and socialize. Marrying young separated me from other women my age who are more interested in dating and parties and snagging their first husband. I'm good on the husband front. Astronomy and nuts are my life, but I desperately need someone to talk to.

I don't have any friends and admitting that fact stings. Sure, I have plenty of acquaintances and can hold a conversation, but it's been years since I've connected with anyone—Nick and I connected, or at least I thought we did, and then we were ripped apart because of my stupid indiscretion with Branson. An indiscretion that left me with nothing in the end.

Nick's kiss, though...I swear he felt it too—I'm sure I saw it in his eyes—felt it on my lips.

My fingers move to my lips, caressing them, remembering the feel of his lips against mine. There were so many things I wanted but never got the chance to experience while married to Branson. For one thing, he rarely kissed me, and when he did feel the need to be affectionate, it was always uneventful, unmoving.

I *need* love, passion—the burning kind, the kind I feel in Nick's presence.

"You came out here to see Orion," I whisper, reminding myself that this would be one of the last good gazing nights left before the mid-summer heat takes over.

Approaching my telescope, I get back into the zone. Time flies when hypnotized by the heavens. Any embarrassment for my wild behavior with Nick quickly dissipates and relaxation and appreciation for the vast universe takes over.

A million Sundays worshipping in church would never bring me as close to God as stealing a glimpse at the space beyond earth. Seeing it opens the mind to the limitless possibilities that life has to offer. All problems seemed miniscule in comparison.

I never want to leave after a night of gazing, and tonight the temperature is perfect with just enough wind to keep the bugs at bay, so I decide to stay and sleep under the stars. I retrieve my blanket, lay it flat on the ground beneath a nearby pecan tree, and Rigel joins me. We snuggle while I stroke his long floppy ears, easing us into a peaceful slumber.

Chapter Fifteen

Three days and nights passed without a word from Nick. It's rained steady since our night under the stars. The weather makes it impossible to get any work done on the farm, so I've stayed indoors, busying myself with housework while stewing.

I know Nick is working, but it frustrates me that he's made no attempt to speak to me. He could have easily stopped by the house to check on me, as he does whenever the weather gets crazy, but this time he didn't.

No phone calls, no texts, nothing.

He's purposely avoiding me, and it infuriates me to no end.

The weather has finally turned, and the intense heat of the cloudless afternoon sky dried up the rain-soaked land by early evening. Determined to take advantage of the clear sky, I pack up my gear and head out to my usual spot to do some gazing. Mostly, I need a distraction. The humidity in the air weighs heavily on my already burdened shoulders, but I suck it up, welcoming any diversion to get my mind off Nick.

Rigel keeps me company while I set up the telescope and chair. I sit back, watching the stars appear, one by one, until they blanket the sky. Gazing with a bit of light in the sky is exciting, but not as wonderful as when complete darkness invites stars one wouldn't see in a lighter sky.

Hours pass like minutes before I finally give up and prepare to head in. I'm packing my gear when rustling in the grass catches my attention.

I look up to discover Nick slowly approaching. He's wearing a white t-shirt and jeans, looking unbelievably handsome. My hopes rise as I stare at him, wondering what he will say, but he doesn't speak. He walks up to me, takes my chin in his hand, and kisses me lightly. It's sweet, my whole universe changes. Hope swirls through my heart as it pounds against the reigniting of a pulsing inferno that's been burning since I first saw him.

Nick releases my chin and pulls from my lips, causing me to react aggressively. Reaching out, I grasp his shirt, pulling him back to my lips, where I release my passion. His arms encircle me, and I melt in his embrace as his lips tease mine and our tongues dance. Moments later, we separate, flustered and breathless.

He steps back, his expression isn't one of joy—it's torn, broken, and completely out of place given the steam rising between us. Instinctively, I know what's coming next, and my shoulders slump against the weight of it.

"We can't do this." He looks away, swallowing hard. "I came here to tell you that but..."

"But you kissed me instead." I inch closer, trying to see his eyes. "You don't kiss someone like that unless you want it."

Nick sighs heavily, digging his hands into his pockets. "It's not that I don't want to, Zeta, believe me, I...You are my employer. People will talk. I'll lose the respect of my workers if they find out I'm courting the boss. We're too close to harvest to risk another upheaval."

He might have a point, but reason is nowhere to be seen. I stare at the ground, trying to hide the hurt and utter confusion. I want him, this, us—I need it, more than anything. The revelation infuriates me because now he's saying I can't have it. "I don't give a rat's smelly behind what the workers think. I choose who I want to be with, and I want to be with *you*. They're here to work my land, and my personal life is no one's business."

"It's not that simple, and you know it."

"Isn't it?" I approach him, reach up to cup his face in my hands, and kiss him. He doesn't move—he doesn't kiss me back. Heat rises to my cheeks, and I back away, feeling like a stupid fool.

"We can't do this." His defeated tone and stiff resolve burn me.

A frustrated groan blasts from my lips and I raise my eyes to the heaven's silently asking for strength, but then I just snap, my gaze locking on his with intent. "I hate this life! I spent enough time married to someone I had no connection to when all I wanted was you. *We* connected. We *fit!*" He looks away. "This is unbelievable. Fine. Go. I refuse to be with someone who doesn't want to be with me. I *won't* do it again!" Incensed, I gather up my gear and start to leave, but Nick approaches and yanks me back into his arms.

"Damn it all," he whispers before his lips take mine.

I don't kiss him back. I want to, but the immediate ache in my heart takes my breath away. His inconsistency stands between us and although I know he's struggling with his feelings, I'm steadfast in mine.

Anger rises to the surface, and I push him away. "If you don't want to do this, then I completely understand your position, and I will learn to respect it, but don't play with me. You either want to be with me or you don't. Make a choice and stick to it!"

This time, when I walk away, he doesn't try to stop me.

WEEKS AND WEEKS HAVE passed at a snail's pace, and with each passing day, forgetting my feelings for Nick gets easier. Harvest is well under way and going about as smoothly as I think it ever has. He was right about that—I couldn't risk another worker upheaval. He doesn't avoid me anymore and will speak freely about orchard business, but he maintains a strict air of professionalism and never oversteps.

Good Lord above, I wish he would. I wish for it with a passion I can't possibly explain.

Loneliness has forced me to join the world outside my property lines. Mostly, I crave friendly conversation, so I make my first trip to church since before Branson moved out. It's something I've been avoiding because I can't stomach the questions and gossip, but the need for human contact and a connection to faith has forced me to suck it up and attend church.

I soak up every word of Pastor Rogers' sermon and could attribute his advice to my own life. He speaks about forgiveness and moving on, which hits close to home. After the service, I gather with the other members, in the basement hall, for the usual after church social.

Few people attempt to speak to me—I'm a soon to be divorcée, a pariah or maybe they just don't know how to address their pity for me. James is in attendance and has sent me many friendly nods, and I know he'll approach me soon.

I've been avoiding him for weeks because I've been in such a funk over Nick that I can't stand thinking about anything else. I'm barely getting through the days, struggling hard with all my losses. James can't be avoided much longer if I want the divorce to go through.

As my lawyer, James is slick and gets the job done fast. He's ruthless and takes what he wants without apology and given the way he's looking at me from across the room, it would appear I'm on the list.

He's handsome enough with his freshly cut, blonde-streaked brown hair, blue eyes, and medium build. The only muscle on his body hides beneath a few extra pounds, but it looks good on him. So, let's see, he's decent looking, in his early thirties, and he's available. At the moment, all these things intrigue me.

"Zeta, how are you?" Bethany Rogers, the pastor's wife, coos as she approaches. Bethany glows, with her perfectly groomed long tawny hair and lilac sundress that modestly boasts her growing baby-belly.

As with every time I see a pregnant woman, my insides ache with loss. She's glowing. I never got that glow, and like a punch to the gut, my mood deflates but I fight it. Inhaling hard, I plaster a smile on my face and pat the chair beside me as an invite. "I'm well, Bethany. It's so nice to see you." Bethany is one of my favorite people. In fact, her husband Ben Rogers is a steady second. The young newlyweds took over the church a little over a year ago and quickly became welcome editions.

She tosses me a scolding, yet loving smile. "You've been hiding out. We've missed you, Zeta. You know you're a part of our family..."

"It's been...a difficult time and honestly I dreaded the line of questioning, and...the relentless gossip." My face flushes with embarrassment.

Bethany laughs, shaking her head. "That can't be avoided, but now that you're here, tell me, are you okay?"

"I am. It's been an adjustment, but I'm great." My smile is tight, and I don't even know why I'm trying to pretend otherwise after all that I've been through.

"You don't need to lie to me. You've been through hell and back—I can tell by the sadness in your eyes that you are dreadfully lonely."

I meet her gaze. Now I feel pitied.

Bethany's smile widens and there isn't a modicum of pity in it, just friendship. It's the kindest of smiles that makes me feel safe. "Bethany, I can barely stand it. I do so appreciate when you stop by the farm for a visit, but between work and everything else, I'm lonely, so lonely."

"Well, it appears as if a certain lawyer friend of yours is frothing at the bit to speak to you." She nods towards James.

"Oh?" I play it cool, not wanting to come off as conceited by admitting that I'm well aware James is checking me out.

"You're a prized catch, Zeta, what with all your land and wealth. You're young, beautiful and your heart is pure, but keep your eyes wide open. You've been through so much that I pray better days are coming." It's an odd thing to add to a list of compliments, and the distrust of James in her voice is very apparent. Rising to leave, Bethany leans in and gives me a quick hug. "I must make my rounds. You and I will do lunch soon?"

"Soon." I watch her walk away as James steps forward, taking Bethany's seat.

"Zeta, you're avoiding me." He turns to face me, grinning.

"I'm sorry, James. It's been a busy couple of weeks."

"If you keep cancelling our meetings, you'll never be a free woman." A flirty grin curves his lips, and he sits back, crossing his legs.

"Why don't you come by tomorrow afternoon? We'll sort out the divorce papers and you can talk business with Nick. I'd love it if you stayed for dinner too."

"Dinner? That would be lovely. Nick is still in your employ?" His surprise is evident as he cocks a questioning brow.

"Of course, he's great at his job." I'm well aware that James disagrees with my decision to make Nick orchard manager, but I don't actually care. I do what I want.

"A little birdie told me that Ballantine laid an offer on the table for Nick."

"Why would Ballantine do that? He already has Clive and Branson." Ballantine really wants to take me down. I'd die if Nick went there too, literally die, and I'm pretty sure my farm would be doomed.

He laughs. "Seems word of Nick's *great job* has spread. Ballantine runs a massive operation—you know how hard it is to find good management these days."

"James, are you saying my decision to promote Nick was a good one?" I smile, casually trying to hide any emotion about Nick potentially leaving.

"Zeta, you're a big girl, I trust your judgement, but you need to talk to Nick, maybe sweeten the deal a little." There's a dirty undertone to his words which I choose to ignore.

"Thank you for the heads up." I sigh, rising to leave. "I'll see you tomorrow, then."

"Yes, tomorrow." He nods slightly, tossing me an arrogant grin. I can't help but smile back even though he basically trashed what was left of my day.

Leaving church, I'm incensed, driving like a bat out of hell. When I arrive back at the farm, I search the grounds looking for Nick. I have to know if he's leaving, why he's leaving, and if it's because of me. The thought of losing him, creates an agonizing knot in my stomach that's even worse than the one that's been resting there since he pushed me away.

I find Nick alone in the greenhouse, inspecting seedlings. He spins to me as I approach, raising an eyebrow as he scans my attire. I hadn't taken the time to change and am still wearing my floral sundress and heels.

"Nick, I had an interesting conversation with James...Are you planning on leaving my employ?" There's no point in beating around the bush—I'm desperate for an answer.

Nick sighs and gazes off to the side, avoiding eye contact. "You shouldn't listen to everything James says. He's full of crap, half the time."

"Is he full of crap, this time?" I nudge him, trying to catch his eye. "Answer the question, Nick."

"I had an offer. I'm not sure what I'm going to do." He shrugs, trying to be casual but there is seriousness to his expression. He's definitely considering it.

"Whatever they are offering you, I'll match it and then some..."

"It's not about the money." He turns back to the seedling.

"Don't do this. Don't leave because of me." Tears sting my eyes as I cross my arms over my stomach, holding the nausea in. He can't leave.

I grab at him, forcing him to face me. His eyes connect with mine, and he nods, clearing his throat. "I haven't decided..."

"You don't have to worry about me chasing after you. I'm moving on..."

The softness in his gaze immediately morphs into anger. "So that's it...You're moving on with James?"

I never said anything about James. Why would he assume? "James?"

"*Pfft*. Don't act like you don't know. He texted and said he'd see me about the contracts tomorrow after dinner, *with you*."

No doubt, James sent a text. He and Nick just love to butt heads. *Men*.

His jealously elates me for about a millisecond and then I snap, placing hand on hip. "You've made it *crystal* clear that you and I are not going to be together. What am I supposed to do—sit around pining after you? I have a life to lead, Nick. Do what you want. All I ask is that you give me reasonable notice." Straightening, I spin on my heels, and leave him staring after me as I stomp away.

Chapter Sixteen

The nausea didn't leave when I walked away from Nick. The thought of him leaving haunts me—it's all I think about. The problem is, I don't know how to make him stay. It has to be his decision, I know that, but it still sucks, and the suspense is killing me.

Busying myself around the farm takes all my strength, but I do it. The farm is my priority even if my soul is being tortured in the worst possible way. I can't let my birthright suffer too.

James stops by mid-afternoon, as promised. We've been sitting on the porch, sipping sweet tea, and chatting about the details of my divorce. My heart really isn't into it, but I've got an agenda, and I hope his enormous ego works to my advantage. I've no intention of becoming romantically involved with James, but if I play my cards right, having him around might help my situation with Nick. Especially since Nick is jealous of him—if Nick's jealous, it means he cares—I'm holding on to that thought, even if it sounds insane.

"James, would you care to go stargazing with me this evening?" Even as I ask the question, I regret it, but somehow keep up the charade.

"Stargazing?" James laughs as if surprised by my bold invitation. He stares at me, surprised, but my straight face confirms the seriousness of my invite. He shrugs, nodding his head. "Sounds intriguing, I'd love it."

"Well, we are close to dinner. Why don't you head out to talk your business with Nick and then come back to the house? We'll have dinner and go over the final details—we can head out after dark."

"Sounds good." James packs up his briefcase and goes in search of Nick.

I smile to myself, knowing that I'm digging a thorn in Nick's side. He dislikes James on every level. In fact, he barely tolerates James—most people don't, but he's an awesome lawyer, even if he's as greasy as an oil slick in July.

Sending James off to harass Nick brings me great joy.

Yup, I'm being childish, but more or less, I just want Nick to come back to me. I truly have no intention of the dinner and stargazing amounting to anything romantic, but I'm counting on James smugly bragging about the date with Nick. Bragging is James's second language. An evil smile curls my lips—I hope Nick stews in it.

Aside from the business of the farm and my divorce, there isn't much to talk to James about. I struggle, trying to keep up the mundane conversation during dinner. James seems immune to it and is content to ramble on about himself, so I ride it out and continue with the senseless banter.

It's no use.

Wishing for an escape, I curse myself for inviting him out to gaze with me. It was a stupid mistake, and now I'm forced to share downtime with James when all I really want to do is put an end to the dry conversation, I'm currently entangled in.

Desperate to end the evening, I feign distress, which isn't difficult because the thought of spending another moment with James seems like the worst kind of torture.

"James, do you mind if we take a raincheck on the stargazing. All this talk about divorce has sort of brought me down, and I'm really not in the mood anymore. Plus, it's been a long day, and I'd really like to turn in early."

"Of course," he says with an understanding nod. "Another time."

Thank you, Jesus!

A few minutes later, James drives off, promising to be in touch once the divorce papers are filed.

After tidying up, I race upstairs, change into a yellow, spaghetti-strapped sundress, pull my hair into a ponytail, grab my gear, and race to my spot.

Stretching, I let go of a deep cleansing breath—I'm so grateful I blew James off. I set up my telescope, eager to lose myself among the stars. When I lean into the eyepiece, happiness washes through me, bringing with it a sense of peace. Time passes as I become one with the night sky. Orion is exceptionally brilliant tonight. I admire his glorious light, my eye to the universe is exactly what I need—it's as if Daddy is smiling down upon me.

My blood runs cold when arms encircle me from behind, and a man's hot breath brushes my neck. For one terrifying second, my heart stops, my body goes rigid, and the hair on the back of my neck stands up. The pounding of my heartbeat in my ears intensifies as the unfamiliar body invading my space tightens its grip.

"I thought I'd come back. I knew you'd change your mind," James whispers into my ear, before kissing my neck.

"James." I release my breath, relieved that it's only him, but at the same time extremely annoyed. "What are you doing here? I was serious about wanting to be alone."

His arm tightens around my torso while his free hand trails down my waist, grasping my dress, and pulling it up towards my hips.

"Don't be coy, Zeta. I know you want me." His lips trail my neck, and I catch the stench of his gin-soaked breath. He wasn't drunk when he left, but he certainly reeks of it now.

"I *don't* want this." I struggle against him, but stand firm, determined not to sound like a whimpering fool. The fact that he's here, trying to arouse me is laughable. "Your arrogance is truly astounding, James. Let me go."

"*Uh-huh*." He groans, ignoring my protest as he nuzzles my neck. Furious, I lift my foot and bring it down hard on his toes. Releasing me, he jumps back, fury twisting his face. He growls but he's grinning, thinking it's a game, and then lunges forward, crashing into the telescope and tipping it over. I leap out of the way, but he comes at me again, laughing and grabbing my dress, tearing a strap from my shoulder.

Before I can react, I'm shoved aside as a body jumps in front of me and punches James square in the face, knocking him to the ground. It all happened so fast, that it takes a minute for me to realize that my rescuer had been Nick. I stand panting, trying to process the situation while staring at James's unconscious body. The next thing I know, Nick is by my side, pulling me into his arms.

"Are you ok?" He grips my chin, lifting it to meet his gaze.

My strength, the last drop I had been clinging to, dissolves. I shake my head as tears began to flow. It's then that a new worry crosses my mind, and I look past Nick at the telescope. Pushing him aside, I rush over to assess the damage. Thankfully it's brass, so it's tough as nails and there's no damage to the lenses. I pick it up, release it from the mount, and pack it into the case. Tears blur my vision, but I silence the desire to sob and focus on the task in an attempt to forget what just happened.

It's no use. I tempted fate and created a nightmare situation for myself. I'm not convinced that James would have raped me, he was really too drunk to fight me, but the what could haves are twisting through my brain at an unreasonable rate. I'm not surprised by James's behavior, but it isn't my focus—it's my behavior I'm most disgusted with.

Nick approaches and helps me collect the gear, not speaking. His presence only makes my humiliation that much stronger, and to top it off, his nearness makes the painful longing in my chest unbearable.

"I brought this on myself," I whisper through my tears. "I invited him out and then I couldn't go through with it and sent him home. I flirted with him, maliciously. I shouldn't have done it."

"He shouldn't have come back after you told him to move on." Nick walks over and kicks James who moans but remains down.

"I wanted to make you jealous, so you would come back to me. I was hurt, and I wanted to hurt you back. I wanted to make you mad." A huff of laughter escapes the tears. "I behaved like a stupid reckless teenager and if you hadn't happened by..."

"Well, it worked. I'm mad, but not at you—never at you." He moves to stand before me, staring into my eyes, but he doesn't reach for me.

The intensity of his gaze and my overzealous emotions collide, forcing me to lose all control and sob like a baby. It can't be helped. My heart aches for this man, who won't take what I so desperately want to give.

Dumfounded, Nick watches me collect the gear and walk away. He makes no move to stop me, which only just breaks my heart more.

I sob all the way home, shower, and crawl into bed, crying myself to sleep.

Sensing I'm not alone, I awake in the night to discover a protective arm pulling me tighter into little spoon position. Somehow, Nick knew I needed him. Grateful for the comfortable silence and warm embrace, I relax and snuggle in, feeling safe, even if only for the night.

Chapter Seventeen

I awake to sunlight and an empty bed beside me. Wondering if I imagined Nick's presence, I stare at the pillow next to me. I don't know if I was dreaming, but I hope I wasn't. My heart aches. The realization that I'm in love with Nick comes swiftly and with great strength. I suppose I've loved him all along—I've never stopped. There's just something about him, something I can't live without.

It only makes matters worse.

He won't take the chance to be with me and it is seriously breaking my soul. If my station in life means I should be with men like Branson and James, then I intend to remain single until the day I die.

That day would be an eternity away if I can't have Nick.

My heart aches for him.

He's like my guardian angel, always nearby when I need him, but just out of reach.

I sigh, accepting that I have to make a move. Sitting around pining over him, won't get me what I want. I have to do something about it, or I'll go insane. The decision to approach him is the only viable option. It can't hurt to be honest with him about my feelings. I pray it'll be enough to convince him that we should be together.

On the way out of my house, James approaches his car which is still parked out front. He must have slept where he fell. When he catches a glimpse of me, he stops walking, staring shamefully at the ground.

"I'm so sorry, Zeta. I'm a scoundrel when I drink. It will never happen again." James's tone is laced with embarrassment which is something I never imagined I'd see on his face—his arrogance prevents it.

"You'll understand when I look for other representation?" I say. "You can finish with the divorce, but that will be the end of our association."

"Yes, ma'am, I'll file the papers today, and you will be officially divorced." He nods his goodbye and climbs into his car.

I wait for James to drive away before taking off on foot to find Nick. When he can't be found on the grounds, I head back to the house and wait for the end of the workday to arrive.

It feels like an eternity.

Just after sunset, I walk to the worker cabins at the edge of the orchard. Nick's cabin is the largest of the cabins. The cozy accommodations are part of the manager's compensation. I approach his cabin, knowing he'll be at his desk, winding down.

I creep up the stairs and stand on the porch, staring at the door, trying to work up the courage to knock. Before I get to it, the door swings open, and Nick stands before me. He says nothing but pushes the door open as a silent invite for me to enter. Somehow my legs take me through, my heart pounds nervously in my chest.

I'm petrified but at the same time resolved.

We need to have this conversation. It's so long overdue.

The door closes, Nick spins me, yanks me into his arms, and his lips take mine in a flurry of hungry kisses. I throw my arms around his neck, trailing my hands through his hair, and holding him to me.

What was it I needed to say?

I can't make sense of Heaven or Earth, not now.

And then he pulls away, and again I see the regret plastered all over his face and just like that, I'm gutted.

"What can I do for you, Zeta?" He tries to sound casual, but darkness crosses his face, changing his demeanor. He closes himself off as if he didn't just kiss me into oblivion.

Stunned, I gape at him, my jaw on the floor. "You know why I'm here. Why can't you just take the chance to be with me?"

"I want to be with you..." Nick sighs and walks past me to his couch and sits, burying his face in his hands. "We just shouldn't. I can't."

A little piece of me suspected this much but hearing him say the words, yet again, hurts more than I expected. I was sure he'd have a change of heart. Clearly, I was wrong. Burning agony flashes through my body and mars my soul.

The thought of Nick not loving me the way I so desperately love him never crossed my mind, until now. I know it's crazy, but I need him to know that I love him more than a position in society, more than anything, so much that I am willing to fight for it.

"I love you, Nick." I choke on the words as tears escape my eyes. "All these months, all this time—I never stopped loving you—I swear to God, I never will."

Nick raises his head. His tormented eyes connect to mine, and I see it, I understand everything now. It wasn't position holding him back, it was fear...of what I can't imagine, but seeing the pain in his eyes forces me to accept his words.

I never want to cause him a moment's pain. I'll be alone forever if it means he isn't hurt. That look on his face, it's killing me.

Nodding my acceptance of his resolve, I turn to leave, but before my hand reaches the doorknob, I'm yanked back into his arms and his lips take mine. Relief washes over me as we kiss, but more tears escape my lids. Confused, I pull away and look into his eyes, demanding an answer.

"I *know* you love me, too." I tilt my head in question.

His hands trail up to my face, cupping my cheeks. He nods. "You deserve so much more than—"

"Than what?" I snap, slapping his hands from my face. "A man who actually *loves* me? Someone who makes me feel things I never knew existed? If you love me, then you can't throw this away. You can't!"

"I just need time to figure this all out..."

Irrational anger rises, flushing my cheeks, causing me to strike out with words I know aren't true. "So that's it?" This sudden rage takes over all reason, I'm seething with it. Nick's eyes soften, and he shakes his head. He reaches out to me, but I shirk his touch and speak before he has a chance to argue. "I can't do this..." The words hurt as they come out, stabbing me in the heart, but I say them—I can't stop myself. "The pain—it's—you should have just left me alone. You should never have come back."

"Zeta..." His voice cracks but I can't stop myself.

"No! I can't believe you're jerking me around, again! I can't do this anymore. You need to take that job. I can't keep going back and forth like this—it's killing me."

Furious, I push him away and race out the door, slamming it behind me. I hear the door open as if he might come after me, but I don't give him the chance to catch me. I race, as fast as my legs can go, back to the safety of my house and then cry myself to sleep.

Chapter Eighteen

Three long and torturous days passed—every second drags like a knife across my heart. Nick never came to me. It both breaks my heart and infuriates me, even though I basically told him to leave me alone. Flinching, my words play over again in my mind.

I told him to take the job!

What was I thinking?

Why did I have to behave like such a crybaby?

I was so angry, but with each passing moment, my anger grows less and the intensity of my sorrow increases. I can't stand anything. I can't eat, barely sleep, although I stay in bed all day, and tears come at the most unexpected moments.

Life seems pointless if I can't be with Nick.

I couldn't even rejoice when the call came telling me that I'm officially divorced from Branson and free to move on.

It doesn't matter. I'm every bit a prisoner now as I was while married to Branson. When will I finally be free? Will I ever have love?

Nick's stupid manly pride overpowers our love. It doesn't make sense—we aren't living in the stone ages. People cross social barriers all the time. The thing is, you either want to be with someone or you don't, and he clearly doesn't.

Maybe he was lonely and just needed something, but he made me fall for him. He awakened something inside me and then turned his back on it, leaving me to suffer in the ruins of a shattered heart.

Well, I won't have it. I won't spend a single moment more with someone who messes with my heart. Life's too short, although at the moment, each second away from Nick seems like an eternity.

Ugh!

The yo-yo of emotions drains me to the point of exhaustion.

It's in this moment that I feel a different longing in my soul—the need to open myself up to the universe. Forcing myself out of bed, I shower and dress in a linen sundress.

Tonight, I'll gaze upon the heavens. It's exactly what I need. The sky is clear, and in a few minutes, I'll be standing beneath a blanket of stars, and Orion. It's the only thing that can ease my mind and perhaps help me forget the loneliness that plagues my soul.

I arrive at my usual spot and set up, but a nearby rustling in the grass, grabs my attention before I have a chance to gaze into the eyepiece.

I know it's him. Irritated, I spin, prepared to lose it but soften the moment I see him. I literally don't have the strength to argue. Not with him.

My head tilts slightly as I arch an expectant eyebrow.

"I came back for you," he says, walking towards me. Noting the look of confusion on my face he adds, "after *the* phone call."

My eyes widen. "*What?* When? I didn't see you."

"I saw *you*, getting married to Branson. I watched, and I knew you didn't want it—it was all over your face, but I let you go." His voice cracks with emotion.

His words gut me.

Tears fall, pouring from my eyes like a fountain. He came back, had I known...

Wait.

He *loves* me. The realization takes my breath away. I try to speak, but a sob escapes instead. He pulls me into his arms, holding me as he continues to shatter my wall.

"When I graduated, I took the job with Old Man Carson, so I could be close to you—keep an eye on you. I needed to know you were ok." I pull back and look into his eyes, stunned.

His words, they're everything I never knew I needed to hear. "You do love me." It pops from my mouth and sounds needy, desperate, but quite frankly I am, desperate for him.

He laughs. "I've loved you all along, Zeta. It's been killing me, knowing you have all this, and I have nothing to offer you."

I place a hand on his chest and look him dead on. "*This* is everything I want."

The space around us suddenly gets brighter and I note several workers with lanterns walking towards us. Stepping back, I watch them appear from the orchard, one by one, and form a semi-circle around us. Confused, I glance at each worker, trying to figure out their intentions. Relief washes over me as I note the looks on their faces. They aren't hostile, they're happy, but I don't understand why. And what's with the lanterns? No one uses lanterns anymore.

I turn, taking them all in, wondering what they want, when Pastor Rogers, appears next, dressed in his white Sunday robe. I spin back to Nick who beams—it warms my soul and more tears spring from my eyes as he drops to his knees before me, taking my trembling hands in his.

"The only way to make this right is for you to be my wife, my partner, my equal." Nick smiles, looking into my eyes.

A sob escapes my lips. "Nick..." I'm lost for words.

"I love you, Zeta, and I can't bear another second on this earth without you by my side. I can't be without you again, so let's do this right."

I kneel to his level and nod as he pulls me into his embrace. So many questions enter my mind, but none of them matter. I'm going to marry this man and never look back.

From behind us, James speaks up, and I turn in his direction. "We pulled some strings to get the license and Nick asked that I draw up a pre-nup in preparation of your marriage. All you have to do is sign, and you and your farm will be safe."

The fact that Nick went to James for help blows my mind. He thought of everything.

He truly loves me.

It's all like a dream, and I never want to wake from it.

Knowing that I'll *never* divorce this man, I turn my gaze back to Nick and shake my head. "No, I won't need it..." I laugh, so happy it seems unreal, but I've got forever in my arms, nothing else matters.

"You have to sign, Zeta. I won't have you any other way." He needs me to know that it isn't my land or money he's after. He wants *me*.

Nodding, I rise, taking Nick with me, and sign the papers.

Then Nick leads me to Pastor Rogers, who stands next to my telescope. Rigel bounces over and takes his place between us, his big dopey face scanning from Nick to me as if he's telling us, "it's about time."

Hand in hand, we say our vows under a blanket of perfectly aligned stars, and I swear, I can feel Mamma and Daddy smiling down on us.

∞ ∞ ∞

Connect with Carys

Thank you for reading *Better Days*.
Sign up for my newsletter[1] to be apprised of upcoming sales
and releases: https://bit.ly/CarysReedRomance
Good, clean, heart-warming romance—What's better than
that?

---

1. https://mailchi.mp/b69456973d76/carys-reed